ADVANCE PRAISE

"*Famous Baby* is inventive, hysterical, and touching. Karen Rizzo wraps a timeless drama about the love between mothers and daughters in a fresh, snappy package for the social-media age."

— Christina Schwarz, author of *Drowning Ruth* and *The Edge of the Earth*

"This deft first novel [is] a satirical exploration of the modern American family...Rizzo's wicked takedown of 'mom bloggers' concludes on an unexpectedly but convincingly sweet note, making this a very pleasing debut."

— *Publishers Weekly*

"In her funny and touching new novel, Karen Rizzo deftly unpacks the fraught world of mothers and daughters, skewers the vast narcissism of the blogosphere, and reveals the emotional wages of unbridled ambition. An enjoyable and surprising ride to some places I didn't expect to go."

— Seth Greenland, author of *The Angry Buddhist* and *The Bones*

"Hilarious, moving, and v   ous Baby* is a laugh-out-loud funny   the modern family in these TMI

— Wendy La   uthor of *Chanel Bonfire*

"Karen Rizzo's writing is so good I want to read it out loud and pretend it's me who is so cunning, sublime, and full of light. *Famous Baby* is a sturdy tale of exceeding relevance that dwells squarely in that nearly impossible landscape of everything so darkly funny and achingly true."

— Marc Parent, author of *Turning Stones: My Days and Nights with Children at Risk* and the writer of the popular, long-running *Runner's World* column "The Newbie Chronicles"

FAMOUS BABY

a novel

BY KAREN RIZZO

PROSPECT
·PARK·
BOOKS

Published by Prospect Park Books
969 S. Raymond Avenue
Pasadena, California 91105
www.prospectparkbooks.com

Distributed by Consortium Book Sales & Distribution
www.cbsd.com

Library of Congress Cataloging in Publication Data
Rizzo, Karen.
 Famous baby / Karen Rizzo.
     pages cm
 ISBN 978-1-938849-30-5 (pbk.)
 1. Mothers and daughters--Fiction. 2. Bloggers--Fiction.
 3. Grandmothers--Fiction. 4. Revenge--Fiction. 5. Family life--Fiction.
 I. Title.
 PS3618.I974F36 2014
 813'.6--dc23
                              2013039662

Cover design by Howard Grossman.
Book layout and design by Amy Inouye, Future Studio.
Printed in the United States of America.

In memory of Bea and Tony Rizzo

Before the "Reality" moms, before the blogs by AngryMoms, GoddessMoms, and PostpartumMoms, before the books by Uncensored, Bad, Drinking, and Tiger Moms, there was Ruth Sternberg, the First Mother of Mommy Blogging—or, as Ruth's eighteen-year-old daughter prefers to call her, the First Lady of Cyber Exploitation...

PROLOGUE

September 13, 2:45 PM

Mom they only have dial up

Are they Mennonite????!!!!

It's really rural…we're in town now. I'm staying a little longer. The organic farm is sweet. They use cotton patch geese and bioherbicides. I'll call soon. Xo

How do you know this Kaitlin? And where in Montana are you exactly???!!!

I told you, M.I.T. science camp? Remember her dad had the black Elvis hair and her mom had tattooed legs

They all had black hair and tattoos and compost heaps and f-ing chickens. When are you coming home?????!!!!!!!!!

!!!!!!!!!!!!!!!!!!!!!!!!!!??????????

Don't talk to me like I'm an idiot please!!

It's a road trip. Be thankful I haven't left the continent. You encouraged me, remember. You said I should takea year off befor

Before college

You were 12 when I said that! And I didn't mean you should stay away this long!

What did you mean?

Honey, there's so much going on here!!

I know. I get your tweets. I read your blog. I'm going to Alaska

Skype!!! Can we just Skype????

I hate skype

For me. For your mother. Skype!

...

November 11, 5:23 PM

Abbie!! Answer me!

Please!

Mom please don't get hysterical we just talked

Where are you???????!!!!!

I'm in Hartford. It's cold. But pretty. I'm spending TDay with Josh and his family

Josh??!!

Becca's cousin, remember? You said he looked like M Cera

But he doesn't

Are you two dating???

He's gay. Love you

Abbie?

Yes Ruth?

Will you be home for my birthday?

You have to come home

I'm 18

That is not an answer

Abbie?

...
Abbie????

Honey??

How was New Orleans?

I'm taking yoga

I'm getting a rescue dog

I'm going to drive off the Angeles Crest Highway!!!!

Please call

!!!!!!!!!!!!!!!!!!!!!!!!!!!!!!!!!!!!!!!

one

RUTH

blame Mary Lou fucking Retton. I blame her for raising the bar for teenage girls, for singlehandedly altering the consciousness of an entire generation of women and effectively ending any chance I had of becoming someone my own daughter would like.

Like me, you couldn't have been sixteen the summer of 1984 and, having witnessed that imperturbably ecstatic, muscle-bound spark plug beat out her competition with inhuman ease, been happy selling "Greet the Tall Ships" T-shirts on a hot Long Island beach boardwalk. Watching Mary Lou on TV those nights confirmed the existence of God, life on Mars, and the possibility for happiness. Mary Lou. Me. Mary Lou and me. She was the darling of the 1984 Olympics, the winningest American female gymnast in the history of those games. And I...I was the Jones Beach concession-stand cashier with the most pathetic sales that summer. Piled beside me was my tower of small to extra-large white T-shirts announcing the coming of the Tall Ships, sailing from every port in the world to New York's East River in celebration of America's independence. At the far west end of the beach I sat, the keeper of those silk-screened beauties. Come, celebrate, greet the Tall Ships! *Those tall fucking ships.* I wore one of those shirts every single day and scribbled down my personal sixteen-year-old suburban-girl angst in the diary that I carried everywhere that summer—a tiny felt journal with a faux-fur tiger on the cover. I had no choice but to scribble—if I'd *had* a choice, I would have been Mary Lou Retton. Or Missy Cataldo—my best friend Missy, with the Playboy Bunny breasts, steel-reinforced thighs, and impossibly thick mane of hair pulled back in a ponytail that was bleached green from daily swim-team practice.

Among the junior lifeguards at Jones Beach that summer, Missy held the distinction of spotting the most drowners—those beachgoers who insisted upon dog-paddling too far out into the cold ocean, only to cramp up and sink. Behind her killer stack and Chlorine Barbie looks, Missy was a brain, and the only other kid in Mr. Harris's tenth-grade English class, aside from me, who knew that "four legs good, two legs bad" referred to a need for unity in the face of oppression and not a wrecked gateleg table. She had a dumb-smart Judy Holliday kind of laugh that she perfected by watching *Born Yesterday* over and over, and I was the girl who actually knew who Judy Holliday was.

Connie was the third member of our group, although

we weren't really a group, just three beach-weary com-
patriots and veterans of the same disbanded Camp Fire
Girls troop. Connie was working her third summer at the
concession stand down the boardwalk from me. She was
already looking forward to attending some Ivy League
college that was known to have the worst winters and
most freshmen suicides of any school on the northeastern
seaboard. That summer, Connie already couldn't wait for
it to be *next* summer, when she'd be seventeen and able
to quit her "stupid beach existence," as she called it, and
intern in an air-conditioned office somewhere in midtown
Manhattan, where she imagined wearing support pantyhose and taking cigarette breaks at the water cooler. She
was anxious to start down the road she was convinced
would lead to her becoming the first female governor of
New York. But that summer, she was stuck working the
East End concession stand. She sat on a stool inside one
of the cool, cavernous beach buildings, beside one of a
half-dozen ancient manual cash registers with the drawer
wide open, ringing up purchases while following the
principle of "one for them, one for me." Connie kept track
of all those *one for mes* inside her own electronic cash-
register brain. She'd smile winningly at the concession
managers, the mothers in skirted swimsuits, and the kids
with third-degree sunburns, and then ring up *one for them
and one for me, another one for them and another one for me.*

"You're crazy—how do you do it?" I asked her in the
echoing din of sandy, shuffling feet and screaming children.

"It's easy," she shouted back. Reaching into the freezer,
she grabbed two ice cream push-ups and tossed them in

front of me. Then she rang up one for forty-five cents and, smiling brightly at me instead of ringing up the second one, said, "Ninety cents, please." Since the forty-five cent total was hidden on the broken display, and Connie's smile was so bright and genuine, the customer usually handed her the ninety cents without a second thought. All the managers trusted her, because she was the smartest cashier they'd had in many summers, and the line at her register was always moving. Her supervisor wanted to promote her to manager, but Connie demurred. "Oh, no," she said, "I'd much rather work on the floor, interacting with all the fascinating people." Her career in politics was already well under way. At the end of the day, Connie would treat us all to chocolate egg creams and BLTs at the Palms Deli, courtesy of her daily graft.

"Such a generous friend," my mother often said. "You're lucky to have her, and that Missy—such a lovely girl."

But Connie and Missy struck me as the lucky ones: They were perfectly happy being themselves. I was the one who wanted to be Mary Lou Retton.

And why wasn't I? Why, at the very least, didn't my parents push me to study violin or piano or the French horn at the tender age of three so I could at least become a world-class virtuoso? Why was I stuck on Long Island, peddling a bunch of stupid T-shirts while pimply, sun-burned lifeguards made lewd jokes from behind their stupid mirrored aviators? But most importantly, *why wasn't I Mary Lou?* So I scribbled some more, and the more I scribbled, the longer my diary became. I scribbled about everything puzzling and disappointing in my life, eventually making it into a story about someone else living in an alternate-universe version of my New York suburb. It was the fictional version of my life—because God forbid I should reveal anyone else's bloody secrets—and I called it *Mary Lou and Me*. It was my first novel, and it was number one on the *New York Times* bestseller list for longer than anyone ever could have imagined.

Mary Lou and Me was about a girl named Anais, who'd been jettisoned into the dangerous, uncharted territory of high school. In the course of three hundred pages, our heroine survived not only her senior year but also the deaths of her father and her best friend, a near-fatal car accident, and a couple of dozen "humiliating, agonizing—yet, at the same time, oddly hysterical—situations," all leading her to the ultimate realization that it's true, *you can't go home again*; and maybe you don't want to in the first place. It's always seemed to me that the past is kind of pointless, anyway. There's nothing you can do about it; there's nothing you can do *with* it, except carry it around and try to survive it. Given the choice, I've always been one of those people who think it's best to let sleeping dogs lie.

I was twenty when *Mary Lou and Me* was published—my first and *only* novel. I had turned my life into a funny and tragic fiction and actually became my own Mary Lou. But a new problem soon presented itself—namely, topping that literary gold-medal equivalent—and I struggled over my second novel for the next seven years, with no success. Along the way, I fell in love with an infuriating man named Justin and married him—and when I found myself pregnant, the solution to my writer's block became crystal clear: It was simply a matter of taking advantage of my wrecked hormonal state. I soon realized that the angst and paranoia stirred up in the unbalanced chemical cocktail of my imagination made for better reading than any fiction I was capable of inventing. That, along with the birth of my daughter Abbie—my amazing, insightful, perfect child—led to the next big discovery of my writing career: It was easier not to turn any of it into fiction. In fact, I didn't *need* fiction! So it went that I fell in love with an infuriating man, and we had a daughter, and our marriage dissolved, and I scribbled about it all and continued my success as a blogger. And my daughter grew up to hate her mother's scribbling.

That last part—about my daughter hating my work (and, I suppose, by extension, me)—is a bit surprising, because I'll be the first to admit that Abbie isn't an embittered person, though she does tend to carry her privacy to a some-what psychotic degree. It wasn't as though our lives were separate—but unless you're a mother, you can't possibly know how *entangled* you become in your child's life. It's not just the day-to-day tedium, the schlepping, the care and keeping. It's that your child's experiences become your own. It isn't possible to separate your child's hurt from your own personal, emotional reaction to the bullies at school taunting her. Kids don't know this because they're miniature Ayn Rands, deluded into thinking they were born perfectly autonomous creatures.

It was funny in a way—the more I wrote about Abbie, the more her friends wanted me to write about *them*, offering me their own stories and angst. "Um, Ruth, you wouldn't believe, the weirdest thing, like, happened to me. And like, while it was happening I kept thinking, 'No one would believe it was happening, except like, maybe someone who was a writer, and wrote about things that were kind of weird that nobody else would ever believe.' You know?" Because everyone loves having her stories told—everyone except Abbie. No matter what I wrote about her, I could never manage to redeem myself in her eyes—and the truth is, I couldn't stop myself from writing about her. I remember, after Abbie's second day of kindergarten, she asked me if it was possible to love a person so much that your heart could explode in your body.

"Like who?" I asked. "Who could you love that much?"

"You, Mom," she said.

"No, honey, your heart can't explode," I lied, as I caught a cry in my throat from escaping. "That could never happen."

I knew it could happen, but it would happen to *me*, not Abbie. I already knew that *she* would grow out of that kind of love for me, but I never would—and that terrified me. Writing about Abbie somehow diminished that terror and helped me deal with it—helped keep me solid, keep me from disintegrating into a vapor and disappearing.

You can never make your child understand what it's like to be a mother, no matter how hard you try; you can only love her, provide for her, and try to keep her safe from all harm—at the same time trying to keep her existence from completely replacing yours. Just know that none of this precludes the possibility that your child may abruptly leave you one day, taking a large chunk of your heart with her—or perhaps committing a federal offense in retaliation for all your efforts.

two

ABBIE

I didn't kidnap my grandmother. Seriously, like at eighteen I'm suddenly going to be exhibiting some borderline-personality thing after a lifetime of being the poster child for "Girls Go Science!" I definitely didn't take Grandma by force. She came of her own free will, seeking an adventure, a change of pace, and an opportunity to spend some quality time with her favorite (and only) granddaughter.

Right now Grandma's really tired, so she seems a little dazed. I mean, just because an eighty-five-year-old woman is dazed doesn't mean she's senile. Like I said, she's just tired. And I don't blame her, because the trip here was long, and she needed her walker to drag herself to the bathroom of nearly every gas station on the desert highway between Los Angeles and Tucson. She's tired because she couldn't sleep. She would never think of sleeping in a car, probably because she loved driving so much—up until the stroke.

She used to drive with me riding shotgun, the afternoon sun forming our own personal glass-and-steel sauna, the two of us specimens together under the light. Outside of driving her 1988 Chrysler Newport in daylight, though, she hates the sun. I've never seen her with a tan, and she has only one age spot, the size of a nickel under her right cheekbone, which she covers with a white oil-pastel crayon because "it offers better coverage than Estee Lauder could ever provide." She's never looked her age. So even though she's only six months older than when I last saw her, it's kind of shocking to see her finally looking her eighty-five years. There must have been a day recently when her skin gave up and decided it was too exhausting to hold on as tightly as it had been. Grandma has never admitted to being older than fifty-nine, but I've known the truth for a while because I once stole a look at her driver's license.

I should have let Grandma drive like she wanted to—then at least one of us wouldn't be so exhausted—even though she hasn't driven in two years, since the stroke that left her with a pretty useless left leg and arm. My grandmother's in denial of her paralysis. She believes her left arm is still functional. I'm like: "Grandma, can you raise your left hand?"

"I most certainly can. See?" Then she'll playact: "Oh, yoohoo! You dropped your telephone!"

Her hand never leaves her side, but she believes that she's raised it above her head and waved at some imaginary passerby. Her neurologist, Dr. Martini—who is officially my newest fifty-year-old role model—says it's a neurological condition caused by damage to a specific area in the back of her brain, a condition in which the patient can't grasp the fact of her paralysis because another part of her brain that *isn't* damaged tells her that her body is working just fine. Which means that even our brains can lie to us—don't get me started on the implications there. Grandma senses having moved her arm, and she can recall for me the things she's done with it, in the same way that a golfer might replay the detailed motion of a winning golf swing. She has no awareness of *not* having moved it, which, when you think about it, is opposite of the way that some people function when they actually *do* move their bodies in damaging ways—like, say, typing on a keyboard—and then have no awareness of the harm they've inflicted. Not that I'm thinking of anyone in particular.

Growing up, I spent a lot of time with my grandmother, a million afternoons with her in my mother's kitchen, eating rugelah and pound cake fresh from the Village Bake Shop. We'd stop at the bakery after she picked me up from school, which she did when my mother was too busy working on a book, or her blog, or an advantageous business relationship, and my father was busy conducting one of his meditation workshops or sending a client to some healing astral plane.

My grandmother is the only human I know who qualifies as perfect. When I was small she'd let me spray my iguana Louie with her Chanel #5 perfume and wrap my ponytails in her Pucci scarves. She could make vanilla egg creams like Canter's Deli and a tuna fish sandwich that wouldn't make me nauseous, and she could stay awake for a Friday-night triple feature of old movies, all the while looking like Gena Rowlands—a favorite of hers—in *Gloria*, although we both preferred the Gena in *A Woman Under the Influence* because she looked particularly beautiful for someone having a nervous breakdown. When it became clear in seventh grade that I favored biology over the super-popular film studies and drama program at my middle school, headed by some USC film school graduate who used to babysit Steven Spielberg's kids, it was my grandmother who helped me organize the after-school club Pathologists in Action, which had a total of one member other than me. Grandma acted as our driver to hidden trails in Griffith Park, where we'd crawl around on all fours searching for diseased plants and their beetle predators.

My grandmother, who would never have done anything to embarrass me or anyone else, whose motives I've never had to question, is also, inexplicably enough, my mother's biggest fan. You know my mother, of course: Ruth Sternberg, the celebrated author of *Mary Lou and Me* and two bestselling nonfiction books, the so-called Humble Host of the Full Nest Blog (a.k.a. Life Beyond Motherhood), and the self-proclaimed First Mother of Blogging—or, as I prefer to call her, the First Lady of Cyber Exploitation.

"A real success story, Ruthie is—I'm so proud of her." My grandmother has always said this about her only child, her pride so palpable that even at the tender age of seven, I knew that her idea of my mother was a bubble never to be burst. I knew this then in the same way I knew that certain frightening insects were necessary to protect certain delicate plants. "A survivor," she always said about my mother.

"*You're* the survivor, Grandma," I said not long ago. "What has Ruth had to survive, except maybe giving birth? Oh, right—and being really successful at an early age. I mean I'm sorry I never met Grandpa, but Mom must've had a pretty perfect childhood up until he died. I mean, she had *you*."

"Oh, cookie. Whadayou buttering me up for?"

"I mean it. At least you know how to keep a secret. Ruth must've had it pretty sweet."

Grandma had smiled and opened her mouth to reply, then abruptly stared down, as though her response had become lodged between the floorboards. She's modest, my grandmother—a genetic trait that obviously skips a generation. Which leads to me, I suppose.

🖰   🖰   🖰

I was a famous baby. Like that what's-her-name the test-tube girl. She may have been conceived in a glass jar, but I grew up in one. I wasn't aware of my celebrity until my fourth birthday. That evening, on the way to dinner with Ruth and my dad, we stopped at a store on Beverly Boulevard to look at a Persian rug for my mother's office. Rolls of carpets standing on end like huge totem poles filled an adjoining room. While my parents were occupied in the salesman's office, I transformed into a human pinball, entertaining myself by bouncing off one carpet onto another, then another, then another. Before I could stop, I hurtled onto one particularly skinny roll and sent it crashing into the next one, setting off a domino effect. Carpet rolls fell in every direction, while I froze in the center of the mess, miraculously avoiding the crush. My parents, the elderly rug salesman, and a young couple with a baby stroller all came running in when they heard the commotion, only to stare from the doorway as the last carpet roll hit the ground. There was a moment of stunned silence while the young woman looked from me to Ruth to me and back to Ruth, then yelled, "Oh, my God! You're Ruth Sternberg! I just finished reading your book—*Girls' Guide! Girls' Guide to New Humans!* I bought ten copies!"

My mother and father had both been heading toward me, but the sudden appearance of a fan brought Ruth up short. She instinctively turned toward the woman, who had moved on to me, saying: "And you must be Abbie! You're the *new human!*"

I didn't know what a "new human" was, so I burst out crying. I was crying so hard that everyone forgot to yell at me. Instead, my dad scooped me up while the woman asked for my mother's autograph, and the sales guy whipped out his pocket calculator and tallied up the total for the purchase and delivery of the one-hundred-fifty-year-old faded, threadbare rug that covers the floor of my mother's office to this day.

I cried into my father's shoulder as he carried me to the car. My mother caught up with us a few moments later, scribbling furiously in her leather notebook.

"How do you feel, honey?" she finally asked once we were safely in the car and headed for dinner.

I wiped a long stream of snot up my coat sleeve and said between gulps, "I'm not a *nooman!*"

My mother laughed so hard that snot flew out of *her*

nose, which made me stop crying and start hiccupping with laughter. That was the day my brain kicked into hyper-awareness and I first realized that total strangers knew all about me. Because I am the "new human" from that book. *Girls' Guide to New Humans*...the irreverent, bestselling, nonfiction tome that opened with photographs of me popping my bloody head out from between Ruth's sturdy, pale legs. That was the book that begat the blog, which was illustrated by stylishly candid photos of me experiencing my *normal, happy childhood* at home and at hip, multicultural, child-friendly events throughout L.A. I guess I should be grateful that eighteen years ago my mother couldn't further exploit the birth of her only child by uploading video to her website, if only because she didn't yet have the technology. As it is, it's taken me forever to get used to the fact that pretty much anyone on the planet can find photos of me at every stage of my life somewhere on the internet—right down to those sonogram images of me floating around in Ruth's uterus. I suppose I might have been spared all this if *Girls' Guide to New Humans* had tanked, but even the stingiest of critics hailed it as "brutally honest...better, if possible, than Ms. Sternberg's surprisingly delicious debut confection of suburban-girl blues." That "debut confection," *Mary Lou and Me*, my mother's first (and only) novel, was published when she was twenty. Back in the day—as my mother used to say—*Mary Lou and Me* was the must-read tale of teen angst for girls my age, as well as their worried and confused mothers. I snuck a read when I was ten, and all it did was make me feel sorry for anyone who was a teenager in the eighties.

But it was with *Girls' Guide to New Humans*, which debuted on the nonfiction bestseller lists when I was a toddler, that my mother realized her true calling—keeping people's attention focused on herself by any means necessary. She began by describing, in gross detail, the fluids that were involuntarily expelled from every orifice of her body in the weeks after giving birth: viscous, mucous liquids and bloody plugs...waxy, stinky, and egglike liquids. I used to imagine my mother in her new, post-Abbie body moving across the floor like a slug, leaving behind a slimy trail. Until she threw it out, I avoided sitting on the oversize cranberry sofa in our living room, since she'd claimed to have spent the first eight solid months of my life as a human sieve, leaking and nursing on it round the clock.

My mother wrote about my early penchant for sucking on other babies' toes, my discovery of my sex, my delight in reaching into my soiled diaper in search of something to feed to the cat or smear on my body, my habit of puking at cooing strangers. I mean, too much information, right? (A concept that my mother has never grasped.) But she sure was a trendsetter in that respect.

I know from *Girls' Guide* that my parents didn't have sex for six months after my arrival—and then, for a while, they couldn't do it enough: in bathrooms in Mexican restaurants, in a rented convertible with the top down, in empty hallways. I know that my father never realized he was a closet "boob man" until after my mother began nursing, and that Ruth went into that whole postpartum-depression thing, complete with fantasies of leaving me in a public restroom, burning me like a log in the fireplace, and screwing the plumber while I lay beside her on the bed. I learned about her vaginal dryness, my father's easy, ongoing erections, and his amusing fear of strangers with German accents.

By the time I was eight, I'd learned from my mother's piece on Esquire.com about her secret blowjob daydreams; from Slate.com I found out that she'd been arguing the case of a woman convicted of postpartum infanticide; and from her blog, I learned about the tiny white pills in the bathroom medicine cabinet. A child whose reading list consisted of *Freckle Juice* and *Alexander and the Terrible, Horrible, No Good, Very Bad Day* should not know these things about a parent. Even now, at eighteen, I wish I didn't know most of it.

It was sometime after the publication of my mother's highly anticipated, bestselling sequel to *Girls' Guide*, the *Women's Guide to the New Aliens Among Us (Better Known as Teenagers)*, that I first started planning my post-Ruth life. Evidently my #teenage @Ruth @FullNest exploits and growing pains made for even more #hysterical!, #HEART-BREAKING, and #achinglydevastating!! revelations than the first book. It was another commercial coup for my mother, and basically the last straw for me. Seriously, by the time you're a parent, if you don't realize the consequences of your words and actions, then you're terminally #CLUE-LESS and in need of adult supervision yourself. No one should have to tell a grown-up what's "okay" and what's "not okay." First rule of childhood, right? *That's okay* or *that's not okay.* It's not like I never tried talking to my mother, but some subjects—like the basis of her whole writing career—just paralyzed her. She'd go catatonic, and it's like she'd disappear—no one home. Really, in hindsight, I think I was a little scared that she'd lose her mind if she ever had to stop writing about our lives.

Since none of that can be changed, all I can do now is try to save my ailing grandmother from the same fate. That's why I've brought her to this stone cottage on the outskirts of Tucson, Arizona—and ditched my cell phone in a gas station toilet on the way. And when my mother discovers what I've done, it'll be the reason that she—Ruth Sternberg, celebrated author and First Mother of Blogging—finds herself on the verge of her very own #nervousbreakdown.

three

RUTH

Full Nest Blog
Life **B**eyond **M**otherhood...
Est. 1997 (we're talking 20th century)
www.FullNest/LifeBeyondMotherhood.com

I've just spent the entire morning trying to satisfy my quest for the ultimate yard sale.

First: There ought to be a law against anyone posting signs *boasting* the ultimate estate sale—Moving! Everything Must Go! Three-Family Lawn Sale!—for garage sales that consist of tables packed solely with broken dishes, sad trinkets, and torn plastic

Recent Posts:

- Pinterest rhymes with fetishist

- Don't shoot the ex

- The iPad Thief

- Big ponies are for experienced riders

- Trust me, you don't need it

sandals. People posting said signs for such pathetic fucking excuses for yard sales would be subject to sturdy fines or a thousand hours of community service or, better yet, public flogging.

Second: I got lost and wound up on a dead-end street at the foot of a well-worn hiking path. A sign, yes—"Estate Sale. Everything Must Go"—in front of a huge, neglected California bungalow. The fiftysomething heirs were milling around the, I shit you not, half-acre of rented banquet tables with piles of tchotchkes from the deceased's life (I'm pretty sure they were the heirs, since they all looked exactly alike, save for different or nonexistent hairlines). How could I resist? A faux-Tiffany lamp next to a Fred Flintstone grape-jelly glass next to a mint-condition Louis XIV sofa next to a 1963 edition of *Favorite Fun Recipes for Jell-O!* What did I need? What did I want? I couldn't help but think, "What would Anne Proulx (*The Shipping News*) do?" The answer: She'd likely squeeze through the jam-packed garage to the rat-nibbled boxes of paperbacks in back, where she'd discover a century-old

- Fuck multitasking
- Death be not invisible
- Girls don't need thrones
- Charity does not begin at your mid-century-modern home

About me:

I am your Humble Host and *First Mother of Blogging*, Ruth Sternberg, telling it like it is because that's all there is

book about doll making for a quarter. Then she'd go home and fashion a four-hundred page novel about a cowgirl who inherits a cattle farm in Nova Scotia that will go on to win the Pulitzer.

Third: Good for you who serve only gluten- and sugar-free artisanal organic snacks to your kids and shun playdates where they still "do" dairy. Good for you who safeguard your kids in full-body protective gear for a bike ride in the playground. And good for you who have never allowed water pistols in your house. I mean it. But just know that the minute the kids are out of your sight, they'll probably be eating Twinkies and cheeseburgers, jumping out of airplanes, and joining the Marines.

Fourth: Last but most. My mother. You know how challenging the early Alzheimer's diagnosis was, then on top of that, Mom's recent diagnosis of stage-four uterine cancer. (Everyone, please remember those yearly screenings. Make an appointment today!) I've so appreciated all your support since Mom got sick. It's certainly been comforting to hear of your own experiences with ailing parents and all the advice you've offered me, and I thank you. The fact that I've decided to bring Mom into my home so I can care for her in her last few precious months has really hit a nerve with a lot of people. Listen, I can only answer for myself, and for me it seemed the perfect opportunity to give back to the woman who gave to me for so long to give back instead of prematurely grieving…to try to be "in the now."

The webcams I've had set up throughout the house to record my mother's final stay are only a tiny tool in my efforts to share with all of you, my surrogate family, this particularly personal and intimate experience. What they can't record is the whirlwind of emotions that we all try to keep in check just to survive. I'm winging it here folks. I don't pretend to have any answers, but I can tweet the journey.

Also, I know you've been hoping for news of Abbie. She's certainly right behind this decision, as my mother has been a force in her life as well. There's a good chance she'll be home from her extended trek across the country to put in her two cents. Free spirit that she is, she's never been one to be pinned down, or second-guessed, or told what to do—and rightly so. Gotta let those kids fly, dance to their own beat, etc. Owing to that, the psychic bond between us has never been stronger. I can feel her presence and support, no matter how near or far she may be. And I know that she feels mine.

Alrighty then...

four

ABBIE

I have this weird feeling under my rib cage. I can rule out inflammatory cartilage, because I don't have a cough, and I know it's not costochondritis, because I'm not genetically predisposed, and I haven't had any physical trauma. It could be what my grandmother used to call butterflies in the stomach, but it feels more like a squirrel is whipping up my insides, trying to escape. It's the feeling I used to have after reading my mother's blog, which lately is all about my grandmother, who's now sitting at my kitchen table sipping a ginger ale. I'd have this feeling if I lied to my mom, which, seriously, I've only done under extreme circumstances, like eight months ago when I told her I was taking a year off before college to travel. Instead I rented a tiny furnished bungalow with awesome seventies furniture that really is from the seventies, and I got a job in the one Tucson coffee shop that doesn't require a degree from barista school. I needed anonymity along with some distance from Ruth. I didn't want her to unexpectedly show up on my doorstep in a moment of maternal separation anxiety, so, basically, I've been telling cyber lies for the past six months, which has made me a little anxious. I'm hoping I'll have some brilliant idea of what to do next—like the idea I had forty-eight hours ago to bring my grandmother out here in the first place.

"Come on, Grandma. I miss you. It'll be just you and me…a kind of last hur—" I stopped myself. A last, short, strange, fugitive hurrah is what I could have said. My grandmother finished my sentence.

"A last hurrah, Abbie. It's all right to say. A good idea, this last hurrah of yours. No one I'd rather hurrah with." Then she smiled at me and I cried, cried as I threw her stuff into a suitcase and dumped her bottles of pills in a paper bag—so many bottles, some covered with yellow Post-it notes full of instructions. I hadn't figured on so many tiny canisters. I reached back into the bag and read a few. "Every four hours. For pain." "Every six hours…" "To help in swallowing…" "Twice a day…" "For elimination…" I grabbed Grandma's stewed prunes and farmer's cheese out of the fridge in her small, private, semiassisted living room and put it all in a plastic cooler, then came back for her clothes.

"The green sweater or the ivory?"

"I can't have both?" Grandma asked.

"Pink sneakers or the white ones?"

"You don't got room in that little midget car of yours for both? You have room for my teeth, yes? You don't mind if I bring those?"

I stopped at the front desk to tell the nurse and receptionist that I was staying with my grandmother for the night and that we wouldn't need their assistance until morning. In their nods, I could read what a good granddaughter they thought I was, how they wished the other residents had grandkids who would visit, especially during those long, quiet hours on birthdays and holidays. I emptied Grandma's underwear drawer into a second suitcase, along with the gold and rhinestone reading glasses engraved with her initials.

"You sure we can't stop and see your mother before we go, Abbie? Ruth's gonna be…d…d…" She stopped, seeming annoyed. "Shit," she said. "D-d-disappointed! She'll be very *disappointed* that she didn't get to see you." My mother, of course, is going to be a lot more than disappointed when she comes to check my grandmother out of the Villa Assisted Living Complex to bring her home—she'll be *livid*.

I wheeled Grandma out a back door of the white Colonial-style complex as quickly as I could. Looking back at the building, with its pillars and black shutters, it was like I was running away from Tara with an aged Scarlett O'Hara.

Grandma wants to know where we are…again. Tucson, I tell her. "What country?" she asks, then laughs before I can register worry. "I'm just fooling you, Abbela! I know what country this is, and I know who our fartin' president is as well."

It's quiet here, surrounded by cactus, rocky sand, and the kind of sky that inspires a thousand Facebook likes. Out the back door is a giant drooping eucalyptus tree, the scent of which makes up for the dry cardboard smell in my nose, courtesy of the desert, though it doesn't quite mask the smell of Grandma, which is a pungent marinade of Chanel, old hairspray, and faint, bittersweet body odor. I love Grandma's smell. I've known it forever.

"How is…how is—oh! You know, the handsome one? How is he? Justin."

 "Justin's great, Grandma. He's awesome."

"Why they ended it…we'll never know. Such a shame."

Justin, my father, had his own ways of coping with my mother's self-promotion: He possesses the skill of re-invention. Being with my mother made him realize that he wasn't narcissistic enough to have a successful and lucrative career as a writer, so he became an editor—for a few years, anyway. Then a serious bout of food poisoning led him to become a vegetarian; a broken collarbone suffered in a motorcycle accident led him to yoga and meditation as a way to deal with the pain; and a friend's sudden death sent him to a Tibetan monastery in the Angeles National Forest in pursuit of a life of healing. Along the way, he also happened to realize that he could recognize the psychic conflicts in other people. All of this—especially the last part—drove my mother crazy, and eventually drove the two of them apart. Under pressure, my father became more brilliant, whereas my mother became one of those big black holes that astronomers warn will eventually suck us all up in their path.

"She means well, cookie," my grandmother used to say over and over when I was growing up. "She means well," Grandma assured me after Ruth blogged about how I got my period on her white leather Eames chair. I heard, "She means well" after the teacher meeting, the PTA fiasco, the viral tweets based on *my diary*, and the Wallpaper Incident.

🖱 🖱 🖱

It was my thirteenth birthday and time for me to have, as my mother presented it, "the room of my dreams."

"Wallpaper," she mused. "Wallpaper is so *in* again. There's a fabulous place on Melrose, and they have the most exquisite collection of paper—more like art, art on walls—from all over the world."

"I just want to paint it, Mom. I just want to paint my room."

"Oh, Abbie," she said, "let's go for broke."

It was fruitless to argue with her, because she was relentless in a way that even a kid couldn't match. We went to Lois Knight's on Melrose, a place that served tea and madeleines as you leafed through voluminous books on glass tables, books that boasted "printed and woven fabric designs in imported silk" and "hand-blocked prints inspired by secret ancient techniques from India"—stolen secrets, I suppose—and "elegant acanthus damasks." *Acanthus?* As if the woman in the Ed Hardy outfit next to me is going to know that means "thorny plants"? I liked green, only certain shades, and I hated frilly anything, especially the big Jacobean patterns my mother was oohing and ahhing over.

"Baby, you can paint the ceiling!" she assured me.

I finally found a delicate pattern of tiny paisley in sage green with faded pink accents. It was so beautiful, and so out of sync with everything else in the store. Triumphantly, I showed it to Ruth and was about to tell her what a great idea the wallpaper was, when she said, "Oh, honey, that's so…so, I don't know—provincial, you know? For a teen-ager." I stood my ground, and then went off to visit my father in the mountains for three weeks while the bedroom transformation took place.

When I returned, my mother led me to my room with her hands over my eyes, "Voila!" she squealed, pulling them away. "I went back the next day, to the store, and there was one book we missed, can you believe it? I saw *this*," she said, wildly gesturing to the walls, "and thought, *Well, this is it, this is just fucking it.* It's almost the same colors as the one you picked, but this just inspires that feeling of I'm-here-and-ready-to-take-on-the-world…"

Whose world? I thought, stunned. The world of some evil Disney hooker-queen? My mother had chosen the "Grand Duchy of Luxembourg"—a huge fleur-de-lis print in hot-pink velveteen tied together with brushed metallic kelly-green ribbons that reflected the light from my lamp, which sported a shade in the same pattern, matching my new comforter in a 400-count replica of the walls. Then, of course, she blogged about it—her inspiration and my lack of appreciation. That was the week her FB page got more hits than *iCarly*. That weekend my friend Sophie and her mom invited me to Knott's Berry Farm and Medieval Times. I told Ruth that they'd invited me because they felt sorry for me—because of *her blog*. For a moment, I thought she finally understood, because she looked—I don't know—*pained*, but then she went on an especially illogical rant about bad taste, conservative pundits, and a spike in e-coli outbreaks from tainted meat.

"Abbie, honey, your mother's a good person. She misses you," Grandma says, excusing Ruth's behavior even in my own private reminiscence.

"I'm sure, Grandma."

"She's missed a lot of people in her life."

The only thing my mother actually misses is having published anything decent since I left home without a forwarding address six months ago. Meanwhile, for eighteen years I missed having a mother who could keep just one private moment of my life to herself. By the time I was five, every bit of my life had been uploaded for the whole nosy world of women with sticky toddlers or miserable adolescents who could relate to my mother and her *challenges as a mommy*.

She was the first, I'll give her that much, the grand dame of mommy bloggers, regaling her loyal readers with all the funny/sad/frustrating moments of life with Abbie, the new human (and, later, the alien). Whether I wanted to be the first was always beside the point for Ruth. But the irony is that I was actually close to forgiving her. I don't know, maybe it was getting out of that house, living here in the desert, finding some peace of mind…it all seemed to point to a reconciliation. Until last Tuesday, when I caught one of my mother's tweets, something I try to avoid. But I had a weird feeling. And then I got a call from Grandma.

"You'd be proud of your mother," Grandma said. "I'm going to live with her, and she's going to…keep me company. I don't wanna in…in…what's that word? I don't like special attention—you know that. But she wants to… take care of me."

Once I went online and read her blog, I knew what was up. Ruth wasn't telling my grandmother the part about the cameras in the toilet and shower and above her bed, about the daily descriptions of her life as it reached its end. Looking at my grandmother, I wonder how she'd feel if she found out. I also wonder, if I ever happen to have a daughter someday, whether she'd turn out to be just like *her* grandmother and treat all the people closest to her as the tools of her own ambition? Someone should come up with genetic testing for *that*.

five

RUTH

How the fuck am I supposed to blog without the fucking…
blogee? And pictures, and the Vimeo preview? I haven't
tweeted in twelve hours! *Oh, God, Harry, don't be an idiot.*"

The fact is that Harry's not an idiot. He's my agent,
and he's been my agent since the beginning, from the time
when he was nearly laughed out of his office for going to
bat for a nineteen-year-old girl with the suburban blues
and a novel describing it. He's steered me through the
book deals, movie rights, windfalls, and disappointments
of it all. I can't remember the times he has been wrong.
Is that possible? He's now the age my father was when he
tipped over and died just short of my eighteenth birthday.
I met Harry the next year, after picking his name out of
a guidebook to literary agencies and telephoning with a
fake British accent, pretending to be a writing teacher from
Bennington College hawking a girl wonder by the name of

Ruth Sternberg. Harry listened even though he knew it was
a phony call.

At the moment, however, Harry and I have problems.
Big problems. "Why those yo-yos at the assisted-living
place waited until the morning to call me, I have no fucking clue," I say for the umpteenth time since his arrival.
It's been thirty-eight hours since Abbie ran off with my
mother, and now Harry's here, breathless and unshaven
in my kitchen, pouring himself a cup of cold coffee. He's
looking puffy this morning, mopping the shiny high
forehead under his great, dyed ash-brown coif, trying not
to breathe in huge, worried gulps. He hasn't looked his
age until now, until this very moment. Harold Klein, boy
wonder, is looking his fifty-two years, which is exactly six
years older than me. There's gray in his stubble, which is
probably why he's never unshaven. But I have to hand it
to him: He hasn't gained a pound since I've known him.
He has the same fine shoulders, which have always been
covered in beautiful, hand-tailored suits, since Harry
never succumbed to the trend of fitted T-shirts over
pressed jeans or skinny black leather neckties or bolos
with ridiculous turquoise-encrusted silver buckles. I can't
say the same for myself, although I'm certain I've burned
every photo of me in black kohl eyeliner and blue-spiked
Sid Vicious hair.

Harry's breath smells of too much coffee and Altoids.
When I first knew him, it was Tic-Tacs and Scotch, the
latter of which never hampered his style or behavior—
except for the six months before my twentieth birthday,
after he sold my book. The only thing that may have been

different during our brief fling was that his pants were more wrinkled from pulling them down during all those afternoons in the back of his Mercedes, the front seat being too cramped with the manual stick and all. I ripped his pants once, yanking them down too hard, and I popped the buttons off a couple of his Armani shirts, but I did that on purpose after he put his thumb through a pair of twelve-dollar pantyhose I was wearing for a meeting with my editor. For the first time, sex was intoxicating and exciting and so much *fun*. I couldn't remember having had as much fun before then, not at school, or at camp, or at my first job, or on my first date—not during any of those times when I was supposed to be having more fun than I could possibly stand. Missy had told me that sex could be fun, but I'd imagined that either she was lying or her natural athleticism made it so—or else I was expecting too much. But at nineteen, with my novel sold and Harry, the twenty-six-year-old boy wonder, rutting with me in the back of his silver Mercede*s, then* I was having a good time, like the carousel in Central Park when you're five. Better not stay on too long, though, or else you'll become sick and lose your lunch on your good shoes and never want to ride it again. Suffice it to say, our foray into ravenous, semiclad sex was a brief ride, as it needed to be in order for us to stay together for so long.

"Will you make me a pot of fresh coffee…*please*?" Harry says after spitting out the cold stuff into the sink. "Let's just think here. Just let go of the emotion and think rationally, *please*. There are only facts, the first of which is that Abbie is a very angry young woman who may have committed a felony, if one considers the abduction of an elderly woman in a confused state of mind to be a kidnapping, and that your somewhat dwindling readership—"

"Kidnapping! Jesus, Harry, you're just being a fucking drama quee—. What dwindling?! Like I don't have two million followers and the most popular…like I couldn't write something else if I wanted to?!" Harry gives me a brief pitying look, but I ignore it.

"I'm not talking about you right now, Ruth. Just for a moment, I'm talking about Abbie."

"Right. My daughter with the 4.7-grade-point average, my daughter who gets courted by Stanford and Berkeley, is gonna kidnap—"

"How is it possible you didn't know she was lying about this whole goddamn *road trip*? That she's been in frickin' *Tucson* of all places this whole time? How did that happen? How is that possible?"

"What? I don't know, Harry." This reminder of my daughter's six-month ruse instantly ups my body temperature and turns the back of my neck cold. "I don't know. Those phone records could be fake."

"The guy's a pro—"

"What is he? Homeland Security!"

"Ruth, she's been in Tucson this whole time! Now this guy's trying to narrow down her location, get an address."

"It doesn't make sense," I say, but the words sound like little yelps and tear at my throat. There was a time when Abbie waited for me to read her to sleep, then without warning she was a teenager. I know there were years in between, because I catch the random Photoshop renderings of them on my desktop slideshow late at night, but they happened in the span of a movie, a commercial.

"Makes perfect sense to me. How else could Abbie get away?"

"Get away? Get away?! Sounds like a prison break—"

"You know what else makes sense? That she has Esther and she's going to tell her about the whole setup. What happens then, huh? You tell me."

"Abbie would never tell Esther. Abbie would never say anything to her grandmother to hurt…I mean, worry, you know, cause her any distress…did I say worry? Not that there's anything wrong with recording her last—"

"The second fact I've decided upon," says Harry, "is that we are *not* going to tell *anyone* about the first fact."

"Wh—"

"No, don't speak yet. The third fact is that we have to be very careful here. If I know Abbie, the last thing she wants is publicity—but we don't know what she's up to yet, and this is a situation that could very easily get out of hand. Just think what could happen, Ruth, if Gawker or Huffpo or, Christ, TMZ got ahold of this. Which is why it's crucial that we keep our mouths shut. Do you understand what I'm saying?"

"Harry, I hate when you talk to me like I'm five—"

"Listen to me, Ruth. We are going to find your mother. We are going to bring your mother back here without any brouhaha, and no one will ever be the wiser. But in the meantime, we have *got* to keep a lid on this thing."

"Fuck, Harry—who am I going to tell? Who?"

A wave of fatigue washes over me and my jaw goes slack. It's too much energy to close it. My eyes rest on a tiny cut near Harry's right earlobe. Other than that and his only slightly disheveled appearance—which, for the average man would seem downright put together—there's nothing to indicate that Harry has just landed in the middle of a giant shit storm. He looks good. Maybe I'll remember to tell him that. His hairline hasn't moved an inch. How is that possible? I've always said that Harry has more hair than any man deserves—

"Ruth? Did you hear what I just said?"

"Yes, Harry, yes, I hear you. Okay?"

I've been rolling around a pill in the corner of my jeans pocket. It's a spare that I keep there in case I have one of those anxiety attacks I sometimes have when I'm shopping. I can easily pluck it between my fingers and bring it to my mouth without shaking out my telltale bottle of Paxil. I pop the thing in my mouth before Harry sees my hand move. I should have some food with it; otherwise, it'll make me nauseous and dizzy.

"I'm hungry, Harry. You haven't eaten, have you?"

"Good," he says. "That's a good sign, you're hungry. Now listen to me, Ruthie. *Please,* listen. Please do as I say. If you need to vent, then toss out a couple of tweets, but do not, under any circumstances, even *hint* at the Abbie situation. And I don't want to sound crass, because it's not about the money per se, but as far as your blog itself, your very lucrative blog—you've got your sponsors, your advertisers, those people who pay you inordinate amounts of money, those people at USA who are talking reality series, and they will be very upset if you lose your credibility. Very. You should know that. Please, again, it's not about the money, but it also wasn't cheap fitting the *whole entire fucking house with hidden cameras.*"

"Harry. Please, *please*, don't say 'please' again. You make it sound so fucking condescending."

Harry pokes the side of his cheek with his tongue. He does this to monitor what he's about to say next. "Okay, baby, there is no subtext today. There is only fact—the fact is that you will resemble a horse's ass if we don't find Abbie soon. I'll be back in a couple of hours."

Harry blows by me on the way out. I can feel the breeze from his jacket on my arm. It gives me goosebumps.

Full Nest Blog
Life Beyond Motherhood…
Est. 1997 (we're talking 20th century)
www.FullNest/LifeBeyondMotherhood.com

First: I have an acquaintance named Sandy, a mother of three, God bless her. She maintains the illusion of "being so together," preventing herself from disintegrating by recording everything and anything involving her family. She keeps herself out of the picture—literally and figuratively—instead relentlessly

Recent Posts:

- Pinterest rhymes with fetishist

- Don't shoot the ex

- The iPad Thief

- Big ponies are for experienced riders

documenting her kids' waking lives. My friend Sydney, on the other hand, she bakes. Never baked in her life—not until her son was born—and now she bakes. She comes home from her high-powered executive position and bakes for everyone in the free world and then some. Thirty pounds overweight in Stella McCartney and Jil Sander, she can at least offer her son home-baked goods, therefore maintaining the illusion of being solidly on the planet. She can throw her caring and her deep worry and frustration at the world and what it may eventually do to herself and her child into a bowl of wheat-free rice flour with cinnamon and apples. And then there are those of us who blog. Why do we do it? We do it for the same reasons—to prevent ourselves from spontaneously combusting. Which brings me to…

Second: I appreciate your continual reminders of how I've inspired so many of you to write about your own little Abbies and Andys. What you write is touching, heartbreaking, and amusing. I know that because I'm always trolling

- Trust me, you don't need it
- Fuck multitasking
- Death be not invisible
- Girls don't need thrones
- Charity does not begin at your mid-century-modern home

About me:

I am your Humble Host and *First Mother of Blogging*, Ruth Sternberg, telling it like it is because that's all there is

the blog circuit to keep current on what the latest bug up a new mommy's butt is. Daddy bloggers, I especially appreciate your input. As a matter of fact, in response to Rockerdaddudeman over there on typepad-my-ass. com: No, I'm not old enough to be your mother, and congratulations on that moment when your twenty-month-old vomited his lunch onto your Fender Rhodes and you had the profound realization that you were no longer the center of your thirty-eight-year-old prolonged childhood of a universe. *And, dude, he doesn't* really *prefer your vintage Red Hot Chili Peppers videos over the Laurie Berkner Band.*

Third: I keep thinking back to those sci-fi novels I loved when I was a kid. They always involved a portal opening back through time, didn't they? And whenever I have a day like this, I think how nice it would be to have one of those portals in the middle of my living room. Then I could just jump in and leave my shitty day behind, step over the threshold and go back...back to another day. To a day when I convince my best friend M to come to the mall with me for an Orange Julius instead of going to the party where she breaks her neck on the bottom of a pool. And while I'm at it, I would keep crossing over that superhighway of parallel time until I've managed to fix every broken thing I could think of. But that's just science fiction, and anyone who knows me knows that I stopped craving hot sex with Captain Kirk quite some time ago.

What I want to make clear to all you diaper-and-tell mommies and daddies is that there's an undeniable pact with the devil involved here. That when all those Abbies and Andys grow up, they may look back and be a little pissed off. But know that that's okay, because by the time your little Abbies and Andys are old enough, they'll have probably figured out a way to get even. That's the pact. I understand this, as should you. Consider yourselves warned.

Alrighty then...

My phone is ringing. I've just noticed it. This could be the second or the twenty-second ring. It's Harry.

"Ruth," he says. "I just need to remind you: If you're gonna OD on Vicodin, please don't blog. You get too damn maudlin and self-pitying. FYI."

"Okay. Thanks, Harry." Eat shit. Then I press *publish*.

six

ABBIE

"Abbie?" My grandmother calls from the cactus garden. "Do you have…seltzer water?"

I don't ever remember so much air in Grandma's voice. It's as if her body can't push it out fast enough, when it really ought to be using it more efficiently. It's like she's leaking oxygen.

"Sorry, Grandma—I'll put it on my list." I tuck the blanket on her lap around her knees.

"Do you use this bathtub?" She points at the old claw-foot tub in the middle of my garden.

"Yeah, actually. The guy who lived here before me put it out here because there's no room in the bathroom."

"It's nice."

"Once you get used to it, it's pretty amazing taking a bath out here at night. Sometimes small animals fall in it though, and that's weird. Javelina. You warm enough?"

"Ahhh, nice here in the sun. Like a tulip. Hmmm."

"A tulip?"

"Like a turnover. An apple turnover."

"Grandma, are you hungry?"

"We should call your mother, tell her we're okay."

"I texted her already, Grandma, first thing this morning." Another little white lie, but I can't think of what else to tell her.

"Oh, good. Good. *Text*, that's a nice word. I should've learned to go on the line. Maybe next time. I'm too tired now. Is that why you do the text—for when you're too tired to talk? We should ask your mother. She would know."

"Yes, she would."

"How long have you been here, cookie?"

'Um, about six months, one week, and five days." It's a thing I know how to do—calculate time and numbers quickly. When I was a child I liked to calculate bedtime to the minute. At any time of day, I could tell you how many hours until Christmas, how many days until my birthday. It was comforting knowing that minute information. Kind of like a meditation.

"You're a funny one," Grandma says, closing her eyes, smiling in the bright sunlight. I'll bet she's reincarnated as one of those big Maine coon cats, the kind that lies around the pool at some fading movie star's estate and eats out of crystal bowls. "I can't reach my glasses. Can you?" Her glasses are in the middle of the picnic table. She imagines she's just tried to reach for them with her paralyzed arm.

"Sure, Grandma." I pick up the glasses and put them on her closed eyes.

She nods. "An apple turnover does sound good, though, doesn't it? Maxie liked apple turnovers…scoop out the apple part, eat the pastry separate. Like your mother…"

"Maxie, Grandma? Who's that? Was he a cousin?"

"My…Ruthie's…Ruth's…never mind," she says with her eyes still shut, head tilted to the side as if talking in her sleep. "Naaaah, just…never mind." She's silent for a moment, and then blurts out, "H-how I could be so stupid? Oh, honey, I'm so sorry, Ruth. So sorry. How do you not hate me?"

"Grandma, it's Abbie. I'm Abbie. You're talking to Abbie." I shake her shoulder gently because this is new to me— my grandmother's retreat to a place I can't see. "Esther, it's Abbie. Ruth isn't here. No one could hate you."

"Of course you do!"

My mother made me take an improv class in junior high. She thought it would "help out in life," being able to improvise—like I hadn't been doing it since I was old enough to understand English. It felt like such a colossal waste of time, acting "as if," pretending to be in some awkward equation with a "purpose" and "an obstacle." I preferred calculus. There, the equations had totally clear beginnings and middles and ends. I mean, all of childhood is an improvisation, so who in their right mind needed more? But now, with Grandma talking to me as if I'm someone else, I can appreciate acting "as if." I so hate to admit this, but I'm sure Ruth would know exactly what to say to her mother at this moment.

seven

RUTH

"Sometimes sunsets make me so mad I could kill some-thing," I tell Harry on the phone.

"Oh God, Ruth—" he wails.

"Sometimes they're just this big blazing exclamation of time gone by and nothing fucking accomplished. A farewell party no one's asked for. You know what I mean, like..."

"Jesus Christ, Ruth. Could you stop, just for a minute? Did you get in touch with Justin?"

"We're not talking these days. It's a matter of pride—"

"I left you with two things to do this afternoon. Two things, Ruth. One of which was to get in touch with Justin on the off chance that he has any information. I have no fucking idea what yoga studio he's working out of these days. It was *your* job to talk to him. Abbie might have called him!"

"Acupressure."

"What?!"

"He's doing acupressure."

"Did you have more Vicodin?"

"Abbie's not going to call her father. He's the truthsayer, remember? He'll want us all to sweat naked in a tent or something and make peace."

"How do you know?! You don't know! What are you talking about?! Tell me where he's *acupressuring* at. I'll even go and talk to him. Just—just tell me."

"Harry, I'm going to have an aneurysm."

"Don't do me any favors. I got a call. Call you back."

I should've called Justin, I know, but that's just going to complicate the whole situation further. I can't stop thinking of this *Star Trek* episode, the one with the race of aliens that has evolved to such an advanced state of being that they're all just brains under glass. My friends used to hate that episode—after all, Missy was all body and Connie was all ambition. They thought it was horrible and spooky, but I thought there was something comforting about it, something so expansive yet uncomplicated. If we were all just brains under glass, we'd be less likely to suffer, right?

Now I feel like calling Justin. Justin would be a good diversion. He'd be nice to me. He'd pretend to help or at least pretend to know how to help. It's been a while since I've seen him, though. I shouldn't have had a Vicodin and two lattes for dinner. It makes me nostalgic—and nostalgia always gives me a headache.

Justin gave up coffee ten years ago because it gave him migraines and insomnia. What a pussy. I should give up coffee, but I don't want to be a pussy. Can women be pussies?

Justin may know something about where to find Abbie. I
don't remember the last time I spoke with him—January,
was it? Of last year? When I let him do his acupressure to
try and rid me of the pain in my shoulder from that stupid
ski accident. I told him to leave the arches of my feet alone.
No one can touch my arches. My last shiatsu therapist
told me that I carry my repressed grief in my arches and
that's why I can't have anyone touch them. She said I was
afraid that all my past psychic pain would be aggravated
and released. I didn't go back to her. I did go to Justin,
and *he* touched my arches. Not just touched, but massaged
them with an intensity that should be reserved for open-
heart massage. I couldn't even move off the damn table or
summon enough strength to kick him in the face. I could
only open my mouth in this huge, noiseless, endless gasp.
He knew what he was doing, and he just kept kneading—
and when he was done, he looked so pleased with himself
that I swore I would never forgive him. I could forgive him
for marrying me and divorcing me and being all spiritual
and satisfied, but I couldn't forgive him for touching my
arches. And now I've got to call him and see if he has any
idea about where our daughter has run off to.

Harry rings again and picks up where he left off. "You
promised video—streaming video of your mother. I figure
we can stall things a couple of days, but then…why Tucson,
goddammit?"

"How should I know?"

"Well, since she's your daughter, Ruth, I thought you
might have a clue. Anyway, call Justin. It'll save us some
time if he has the exact address. Then call me. I gotta go. I

gotta call this...*dick*."

"Harry, do you remember that *Star Trek* episode where Kirk is on this alien planet that has brains—"

"Honey," Harry says wearily, dropping all traces of anger or sarcasm, which makes me feel like a child. "Honey, please, I'm on your side, okay?"

"Okay, Harry. I'll call Justin."

"Good girl. I'll be back later. I'll bring food."

I hate it when Harry makes me feel like a child. My daughter, Abbie Antonia Handler, has *never* been a child. I wanted her to be more like my friend Celia's daughter, all dressed in pink and spoiled and demanding, but Abbie's favorite color at the age of four was maroon, and she was always fishing those UNICEF mail pleas out of the wastepaper basket and propping them up on the dining room table next to my weekly delivery of fresh-cut freesia. *Mom, could we give money to a kid instead of buying flowers? Mom, we need to compost; we need to bring home the refugees, save the wolves, rescue the greyhounds, find out why the bats are dying.* It stands to reason that she'd rally to publicize the least isolated human event ever...death, because if death were supposed to be private, there wouldn't be words like *mourning* and *grief*. There wouldn't be wakes and shiva calls, poets and religion, Facebook, Twitter, and blogs. And isn't our fear of dying just the soft underbelly of our need for attention?

Look, at least I'm not denying medical assistance to the poor, or dumping toxic waste into the ocean. I vote. I use LED light bulbs. I donate to ProLiteracy America. I bring croissants and coffee from local roasters to the ninety-nine percent when they do protest overnights around town. I'm like a lot of people: I Google old friends late at night in lieu of making new ones out in the open. My mother has always been proud of me—unconditionally and unwaveringly proud—because I just *was*. Even when she was crazy and medicated, in the midst of her own psychosis, she was proud of me. Most importantly, I loved her. I still do, and I'll say goodbye with an audience of one-point-seven-million if I want to.

I miss her and Abbie and Max and my father and everyone in my life who has ever left me. I hate that feeling.

eight

ABBIE

Grandma, this is Winnie. She's going to help out a little...
with bathing and, you know, personal stuff. She lives
right next door." Well, not *right* next door—down the
driveway and about twenty yards north, my closest neighbor
and friend since my arrival. She's eighty. That's her age.

"You're a little thing," Grandma says to Winnie, who
is indeed not much more than five feet tall, but strong. I
know about her strength, because I saw her pick up her
husband when he abruptly fell out of his chair and died
during dinner two weeks after I moved here. Granted,
her husband, Lou, was even smaller than she, but it was
incredible nonetheless, seeing Winnie cradling Lou in her
arms when the paramedics arrived, his head hanging back
at an angle that a live, breathing person couldn't manage.
So I know she's strong, even though she's tiny and four
times my age—although in ten years she'll only be three

times my age. Winnie's got all her marbles, and she has all but adopted me. Or maybe it's vice versa. She knows who I am and what I've done, and who the old woman with the ghost arm in my kitchen is.

"You could stand to put on a couple pounds yourself," Winnie answers warmly, pressing her firm, bony hand over Grandma's. Grandma laughs, and I pour us all shot glasses of cheap port. "You've got a terrific granddaughter. Sometimes my friends and I even forget that she's not our age. I don't know why she spends so much time with a bunch of old farts like us."

"I'm just an old fart at heart, Winnie," I say.

"I can see a resemblance. Oh, completely. Same chin, same forehead," Winnie says.

"No hips, though," Grandma joins in. "Must've gotten the slim hips from your father. The B—starts with a 'b'... my name, oh, shit! I know I know it..."

"Sternberg."

"Sternberg," says Grandma. "Ruthie and I have hips. Abbie never got them."

My mother has hips and major-league breasts, but she swears that that didn't happen until she was nearly twenty. I'm still waiting. Not that I'd want to look like my mother; I just want to know what I need to deal with.

"Abbie, what was that way your mother described you once? It was so funny. I remember that. I can't remember." My grandmother puts her good hand to her mouth and smiles as though sharing a secret with herself.

"You mean that I look like I came from a grab bag at a drunken U.N. office party?" Straight black hair from a paternal Scottish grandfather; hips from a paternal, hipless Polish grandmother; wide, full mouth from the Slavic great-grandparents on mother's side; dark almond eyes set above the cheekbones of a Mongolian warrior, courtesy of my mother's father.

"That's it! She's the dark version of my daughter…Ruth. You'll meet Ruth one of these days," Grandma tells Winnie. "Maybe when she comes to pick me up."

Winnie and I exchange looks, but Grandma doesn't notice. She's on to the port, sipping it with her eyes shut. "Grappa," she sighs.

"What's that, Grandma?"

"Grappa. We should find some grappa. I used to drink it when I visited the Nabogunda Roondas. I should go back to them. They would remember who I am."

Winnie nods. I must look a little freaked out, because Winnie moves her hand to my shoulder and whispers, "It'll be fine." Then to Grandma: "Esther, you rest and then you'll come and meet the gang."

"The 'gang.' I like that. Like we're gonna…what's that word. G. Grrr."

"Graffiti?" I offer.

"Yes, graffiti walls and break bottles. I like your friend here, Abbie."

"We're trying that stuff tonight," Winnie says to me under her breath. "I don't know why I'm so excited." She winks.

It's a strange thing to consider—the fact that unless I'm hit by a bus or attacked by a rabid coyote, I will definitely outlive all of my Tucson friends by decades. They are my

friends, Winnie and the rest of my Gang of Five. Five
remaining friends, counting Miguel with his pancreatic
cancer and missing left leg. I plan to become seriously
depressed when Miguel dies. He's superoptimistic and is
the adventurous one in the pack. I can see his house on
the horizon, at the end of the moonscape behind mine.
It's the furthermost thing I see before sky and sunset.
Miguel built his stone house and the one I rent, and the
couple remaining in between, back in the 1950s, before
the air-conditioned faux-Spanish adobe ranches with their
expensive, drought-resistant yards exceeded the giant
saguaros in number. We're all going to Miguel's tonight
while his hospice nurse is out.

Winnie and I help my grandmother to my bedroom,
which will be hers for as long as she's here. I'll sleep on
the futon in the living room. Since I don't know any nice
young men within a half century of my age that I'd actually
want to hook up with, my lack of privacy won't be much of
a problem. The thing about it is that I've tried, but I don't
make friends with any guys my age, because I actually feel
about a half century older than they are. The Gang of Five
say that they often feel like youngsters trapped in bodies
that are running down too soon and that they're helpless to
repair. I feel like the oldest woman in town, but in a body
that's still under warranty. In dozens of articles, my mother
referred to me as "the little old lady," "Granny Abbie," and
"the worry wart." Seriously, at five I was worrying about
crosswalks without traffic lights, unsupervised children in
malls, stray animals, premature death, and the fate of the
one-armed man who daily offered to squeegee my mother's

windshield. I worry less these days, mostly because I have less leisure time to dwell on the terrible and improbable than I had when I was a kid. Winnie often reminds me, "Whatever is going to happen will happen whether we worry about it or not, so what's the point of worrying? Besides," she always adds, "you attract the thing you dwell upon." Eighty years of hindsight is a wonderful thing. Hopefully I'll have someone to share all that wisdom with if I manage to make it to her age.

Grandma calls from the bedroom. She's thirsty and wants to know if there's any good "reality" on TV tonight. Winnie calls back to her: "No, honey, it's too early. Besides, it's Monday—not a good reality-TV night."

"Monday?" says Grandma. "I thought it was September. It *is* sea-son-ably mild for this time of year."

I don't know which part of that makes less sense. "Yes," says Winnie without missing a beat. "It'll be much colder as soon as the sun sets."

Grandma appears with her walker in the doorway. "Cocktails on the veranda?"

"Of course," Winnie says, "but just a drop. We're all going over to Miguel's tonight and we've got to be sharp."

"Miguel? Who is this Miguel person? That's a nice Jewish name if ever I heard one."

"Over there." Winnie points out the window into the sunset. "You'll like him. He's very charming."

"Over there." Grandma repeats. "And is Miguel expecting me? I don't want to be an...*in-ter-lo-per*," she says, again overpronouncing each syllable. "I haven't been properly invited."

"I've invited you."

"Abbie, will you be there?"

"With you, Grandma."

"Fine. Then we'll call your mother in the morning."

Winnie looks sideways at me as she helps Grandma to the tiny deck off the living room. She hands us our glasses, then covers my grandmother and me with the old thrift-store stadium blankets woven with initials of unknown game-goers. She sits and covers her own legs with one. The blankets are embedded with tiny prickers, but none of us care. We sit on our lawn chairs staring at the horizon as the sun sets like a blazing orange coin dipping slow motion into a slot machine. It's my second glass of the stuff in an hour, on an empty stomach, and, lightweight that I am, I can feel it. The sky over us turns from navy blue to charcoal to black, and the coin dips farther—dip, dip. I remember walking as a child with my mother, passing a street sign that read "Dip in the Road." My mother said, "Wouldn't it be funny if, halfway down the street, we found a bowl of guacamole?" I remember thinking that no other mother could say something like that. Dip dip dip. The giant coin drops in imperceptible increments until it's a dying line of fire. The port explodes in my ears, disrupting my memory, allowing my body a moment of weightlessness in the dark. The ground buzzes through the soles of my boots.

"Magnificent," I think I hear my grandmother whisper. I think I hear Winnie nod. I think I hear a javelina fall into the bathtub, which causes the spool of memory in my head to restart. Dip dip. Thinking of that guacamole in the road makes my eyes tear.

"My mother never cries," I say aloud, not expecting an answer. It's a couple of minutes before Grandma gives me one.

"You were…little. Eight," she says in a near whisper. "Justin was out of town so I was staying with you…you and Ruth. You wanted to sleep with her. She was surprised. You hardly ever wanted to. I could tell she loved that, your mother did. You two watched…a movie…and you fell asleep on…her shoulder. And I came to the…opening…"—she searches for the word—"the door. And you were sleeping and Ruth's arm was, um, pul-pine-pinned…it was pinned, and she was crying. And she said, 'This is the last time for this. Abbie will never want to fall asleep in my bed again. She'll never be eight and want to sleep in my bed and let me hold her again. And I will never be the mother of an eight-year-old who wants to fall asleep in her mother's arms.'"

That is *so* not fair to tell me that now. But, it doesn't matter. It doesn't tell me anything I needed to know. It doesn't make anything better or worse, even though my face is sopping wet and my nose is running onto my lip, and I feel, suddenly, so tired. That no-man's land between sad and angry: tired.

nine

RUTH

It's true: The best way to make God laugh? Make a plan.

Because my own best-laid plans have gone awry, I've come down with some nasty freakin' bug, so I've had to postpone my mother's arrival for a few days. I was so busy running around arranging things— because I want our time together to be *perfect*—that I ignored all the warning signs, and now I'm paying for it. Of course, Mom wanted to come anyway—said that *she'd* take care of *me*—but I don't want to run the risk of infecting her. So

About me:

I am your Humble Host and *First Mother of Blogging*, Ruth Sternberg, telling it like it is because that's all there is

we've decided to put off her coming for a few more days, and in the meantime I'll be taking to my sickbed in the hopes of recovering as quickly as possible. Which means you probably won't be hearing from me for the next couple of days. But I can't go to sleep now, even though the flu medicine I've been taking has knocked me for a loop, so I've decided to post a few things...

First: This unexpected free time has made me realize that I am just too overwhelmed to see the proverbial forest for all the trees. The truth is that my brain has been so flooded with memories that I haven't had room for the present. I remember my mother circa 1974. I'm very small and she's in her best Diane Von Furstenburg outfit: long-sleeve, black swirl, faux-silk Qiana wraparound dress and matching headband. It is the time before the rest of my life. The time when I was safe. When it was safe.

Second: It's crazy, but I have to say that I'm in love with my new iPad. It has a pink cover (aha, just like my mother's Jackie O dress!) and I love it. Is it wrong to love a piece of metal and plastic manufactured in China? I'm reminded of the first phone I had in my bedroom, when I was fifteen. A princess phone. Mostly my best friend M would call—M, who later disappeared into thin air. I would hold that phone in my hand for hours, turning it over and over, pretending to dial dozens of imaginary friends. M had a powder-blue princess phone, and mine was pale pink with delicate little pearl-like buttons.

Third: Actually, I can't remember the third. Scratch that—I'm remembering too much. I have to go now.

Alrighty then...

Justin, pick up!

It makes me feel unstable going from thoughtful to threatening in only sixty seconds. But Justin actually lets his goddamned phone ring *twelve times* before picking it up—lets it ring twelve times *after* letting it ring twenty-seven times on my first call and then hanging up without even the courtesy of forwarding me to voicemail.

"Finally!" I growl into the phone. "Justin, listen to me: If you know where Abbie and Mom are, you are obligated by *law* to tell me. Not by law, maybe, but by principle. By... by obligation. By—"

"Bye, Ruth."

He's hung up. *Goddamn it, Ruth, don't you ever learn? Ever?* I'll call him back. I'll apologize—no, I won't. Fuck him. *Bye, Ruth?!* Who the fuck does he think he is? No, no, that is not the tone to take. Call back. *I'm sorry, Justin, I apologize. Sorry, but you pissed the shit out of me.* No, try again. *Justin, I'm sorry. I—I need your help.*

That's it. *I need your help.* I call again.

"Ruth, I'm going to hang up again if you start raging at me," Justin says at once. "I don't do raging. I don't *have* to. Understand?"

Understand? Do I understand? Don't fucking talk to me like I'm one of your airy-fairy head-standers. "All right, Justin," I say instead. "I'm just upset. I'm allowed to be upset. Don't some people become upset in yoga if they can't do a particularly stupid—I mean, difficult—move?"

"Ruth, I don't have Abbie's itinerary," he says with exaggerated patience. "But when she calls, I will tell her that you are concerned."

"Not exactly 'concerned,' Justin—fearful. Yes, *fearful.*" Justin is quiet now, but he's still on the phone—I can hear the strains of some kind of Celtic-inspired, Peruvian fucking pan-flute music in the background. He's listening. "I'm afraid, Justin," I say it with just the right amount of restraint so he knows I'm serious, that I'm not simply being a drama queen, that I'm in need of his help. He's always wanted just that, for me to need his help. And I do—I need help. I've got to find Abbie and Esther and bring my mother back here before anyone learns the whole sordid truth.

"Justin, are you there?" Goddamn reception in that goddamn treehouse he lives in sucks. "Justin?"

"I'm here, Ruth. Why am I feeling like I shouldn't trust you?"

"Jesus, Justin, you know what Mom would say to that? She'd say, 'Enough with the feelings!'" The line crackles. "What? What did you say?"

"Nothing. I'm…missi—" The line goes staticky again.

Missy? Did he say *Missy*? "Missy?!" I yell into the phone. "What are you talking about? Why are you bringing Missy up?"

"I said I'm missing what you're saying, Ruth. The reception! It doesn't matter. I can't talk now anyway. I'm hanging up."

"Wait, Justin!"

"I'll call you back."

Missy? He didn't say Missy, idiot. But he'll help me now. Justin will help me now—I know it. I wash down a Vicodin with some Chardonnay in celebration.

www.FullNest/LifeBeyondMotherhood.com

Still up. Still Sunday evening. Still sick. Still obsessing.

I've been thinking about, oh, you know—life, love, the pursuit of happiness. And old friends. It's chilly at night here, and my fingers are perpetually cold after dark. How come some people never feel the cold? They wear T-shirts in the winter, bathing suits in March. My best friend M never felt the cold. She could hoist herself up and out of the water from the deep end of the swimming pool like a fucking porpoise. She'd emerge from her own water pod, bursting through fully formed—a *perfect* human creature. March on Long Island, the air forty-two degrees in the early morning despite the heated pool. I'd meet her after swim practice so we could study together, but I'd always come early just to see her climb out of that pool—me in my red wool coat, hat, and gloves; she in her blue and gold Speedo racing suit, never in a hurry to reach her towel or sweats. Me, shivering; she, indifferent to the cold and wind, walking like a Miss America finalist

About me:

I am your Humble Host and *First Mother of Blogging,* Ruth Sternberg, telling it like it is because that's all there is about to be questioned by Bert Parks on how to save the planet. Happy to be in the water, happy to be out of the water. Happy to be on the planet. Happy to see me.

I was jealous of nothing about M except for her ability not to feel the cold.

Alrighty then…

ten

ABBIE

Miguel's a painter. He paints terra-cotta tiles and bakes them in a kiln in his backyard. Then there's Selma, also a painter, but she only does nudes of young men and women with multiple tattoos and piercings. And, of course, there's Winnie. She was a social worker in the sixties and seventies in New York City...Queens. That's where she and her husband lived until they retired here in the mid-eighties. Grandma's from Queens; they'll have that in com-mon as well. Grandma sold cosmetics, which I guess explains why there were a bunch of cases of hairspray featuring a woman with a beehive hairdo in storage at my mother's house.

Next comes Claire, the crankiest woman on the pla-net—even though, at sixty-nine, she's the youngest of the group. Winnie remembers her from a time before her son was killed in the first Gulf War, before she took to setting out poison for the javelinas and coyotes in her treasured garden, before her diet consisted strictly of bland dairy and pink foods (something she must have picked up from a *Woman's Day* circa 1967). Basically what that means is lots of cottage cheese, vanilla yogurt, salmon, pink grapefruit, and cherry cough drops.

The last of this Gang of Five is Anthony. He's the oldest, next to Winnie. He'll be eighty-six in July, and every inch of the narrow garden around his house is covered in rocks and pebbles that he hand-picked in the desert or on a trip to some country or other. Anthony used to travel a lot, but now he sticks pretty close to home, hoarding only local stones. They either have to be picked by him or given as a gift by a friend. Each rock has a story, though it's not important (or even possible, at this point) to remember the history of each one. The important thing is that there was a reason why each particular rock was chosen: its location, its shape, its size, that reminded Anthony or the giver of something else entirely. Maybe it was a stone in the shape of an eagle, or a rock bearing an amazing resemblance to Gandhi. There must be thousands of those painstakingly collected rocks—and the ones that no longer fit in Anthony's garden line his windowsills and bookshelves, while the best pebbles are given places of honor in martini glasses. That's his other collection, martini glasses—hundreds of them, in every color and size—even though he claims to never have had a martini in his life. He takes his Boodles gin straight, in a Welch's juice glass. Anthony looks like I think my father will in about forty years. He's been widowed for ages, so I asked him once why he never remarried.

"Oh," he told me, "when Marie died, I missed her more

than I could say. But I wasn't old when she passed—not at first. Hah, no one is old at first, eh? So don't think I was lonely for long; it wasn't like I became some reclusive monk or something. I dated quite a few lovely gals. I just waited too long—so that by the time I thought how nice it would be to get married again, I *was* old. Too old. You know, after a certain age, when a man's wife dies, he just becomes so much more pathetic. More pathetic than I'd ever want to be. If a man is young and his wife dies, people feel bad for him—they want to embrace him, set him up on blind dates with wonderful, eager ladies. But when an old man's wife dies, no one knows what to do. They just want to quarantine him because he's so damned pathetic."

So there you have it—the Gang of Five. And then, of course, there's me. Technically, I make it six, but why mess with a good thing?

The Gang of Five knows why my grandmother is here, and they know that she's terminal—their word, not mine. They can't understand why people stopped using that word to mean *not very long for this earth*. Even Claire is being civil: She's just offered Grandma a cherry cough drop. Grandma thinks that Claire has beautiful, intelligent blue eyes, and tells her so. Until now, I realize, I had no idea what color Claire's eyes were. She also offers Grandma a nip from her flask of cheap pink zinfandel, and then Miguel hobbles out from his bedroom with a small, hand-painted wooden box. He sets it down on the coffee table we're all seated around and then collapses into his big leather Barcalounger. No one says anything. Winnie takes Miguel's hand in one of hers and Grandma's hand in the other. Grandma looks confused, and I realize that I should have prepped her a little for this event. I'm about to say something when Grandma says, "Please tell me that's not your wife's ashes in that box."

Miguel laughs.

"Well, Esther!" says Anthony. "How about that, everyone? We've got a live one."

"That's right," says Grandma. "Until I say otherwise."

"Well," I mumble.

"Well, then," says Anthony.

"Oh, for chrissake," says Claire, leaning forward and flinging open the box. A big tuft of dry, purplish weed lies next to a pack of rolling papers. "It looks kinda like sage, but it doesn't smell as good," Claire says, poking it. "Ooh, like shit—it smells like *shit*!"

"I think it smells pretty good," says Winnie. "And it's purple—is it supposed to be purple?"

"Yes, ma'am," says Miguel, looking pleased with himself. "That's why they call it the Purps—either Purple Urkel or Granddaddy Purple. Or maybe both—I don't know. I got it from some kid who grows for cancer patients in California. He says the purple color is the big thing these days; he says it has 'bag appeal.' They got a language all their own, these pot people. But I got it for cheap, because this batch has seeds."

"It's not supposed to have seeds?" asks Anthony, with a collector's interest.

"These days, no. See, you only smoke the female plants, because those are the ones that get you high. The grower keeps the males away from the females, and the females end up pining away for their lost mates and producing loads of resin crystals. And that's the part that gets you stoned. They call it *los rasgones de la virgen*," Miguel adds in beautiful Spanish. "The virgin's tears."

"How sad," says Selma.

"Not so sad in this case," says Miguel. "Some male plant ended up sneaking into the garden and having his way with these ladies. And I got a discount."

"So now what?" Winnie asks. "I thought it would be all ready to go. Do we have to make our own cigarettes?"

"My dear Winnie, I am a *tradicionalista*. It comes like candy now, wrapped in colored paper and gift bags, but this is the way we used to do it." Miguel picks up the pot and hands it to me with a flourish. "You clean. I roll. That a deal? Back in the day, we'd pull it apart and separate the seeds on album covers. See, you spread the leaves over the open cover. The leaves don't roll around, but the seeds do; then you shake it gently so the seeds fall into the fold. It is most genius."

Miguel hands me a pristine record album with Bing Crosby and a very young David Bowie on the cover. I open it and follow his directions. It kind of reminds me of separating seeds from chaff at organic farm camp. I crinkle the leaves onto the cover. Something about how the seeds all seem to know what to do makes me instantly happy. Like they know they've got to head for the fold. *Head for the fold, head for the fold!*

"They say it helps the nausea," Grandma says out of no-where. "And the emotional pain." She turns to me, "Are we all smoking marijuana tonight, Abbie?" I nod. "What fun friends you have!"

I put down the album and hug her. Winnie turns her head and wipes her eyes. Miguel closes his for a moment, while Claire busies herself by popping another cough drop. I pick up the album and finish my job, then brush the cleaned leaves together and place the open cover on the table in front of Miguel.

"Lovely," he says.

"God!" Selma says, "I haven't been this damn excited since I knew I was going to have sex with the butcher at Harmony Farms!"

"Oh, Christ, Selma," says Claire, shaking her head.

"I did!"

"Jesus Christ!"

"No, really!"

For a moment, we all laugh. Claire is the first to stop, her brows abruptly furrowing, causing large folds to crease over many smaller ones, creating a high, hound-dog forehead above wide eyes. One by one, my elderly friends assume the same expression as they each visualize the Harmony Farms Casanova in his bloodstained apron, surrounded by pig carcasses suspended upside down in the walk-in freezer, trying to fend off the amorous Selma...

"We're ready!" Miguel sings, ushering us out of our private Saturday matinees.

We're all going to get stoned together, and for a good cause. Maybe it'll help Miguel's nausea; maybe it will ease, if only for a short time, the real psychic pain that would scream like a coyote if pain itself had a voice. Help relieve the pain that I sometimes see on my friends' faces, if only for brief, subtle moments, as they contemplate the next death—because there's always one lurking around the corner. And they have categories for them. There are the good deaths and the bad ones. The good deaths are aided by family or friends, or both, with some understanding and acceptance of the end. The bad deaths are the ones suffered alone, unattended by loved ones, resisted until the last frightful moments. There are also the accidental ones, but even they can be sorted into good and bad.

Miguel drops some leaves onto a folded square of rolling paper. Deftly, he rolls it up and slides it across his tongue, then blows it dry as though he's twenty and blowing in the ear of a pretty young girl. I see him, for less than an instant—literally *see* him—in that moment of sensual love, and it catches me by the throat. He was beautiful once, Miguel was, before his cheeks became so hollow as to accentuate his bone structure, betraying the mechanics of his jaw as he opens and closes it to speak. There's a photo of him in a pressed white shirt, his long black hair wrested back into a ponytail, loose strands blowing across his face, his skin tan and perfect as he stands next to an equally beautiful Mexican girl in a sleeveless cotton dress cinched stylishly around her waist, her long fingers holding her collar up at the neck. They are standing in front of this very house, except that it's like 1960 and they're young and I'm probably swinging on a star somewhere, awaiting my turn for a body. Or maybe I'm in another disguise, the one I had before this one. Maybe I'm the girl in the photograph— Miguel's wife before she died, long before I was awarded this body in a lottery on a cloud above West Los Angeles. Weirdly enough, I suddenly find myself standing right in front of the photograph, without knowing when I stood up and walked over to it. There they are: Miguel and Carmen. There they always are. But this time, she winks at me. Yeah, that's right—the girl in the photograph winks at me.

Miguel is taking a long, luxurious hit from the joint just a few feet away.

"Hold it in," Winnie says. "That's what you have to do."

I return from the picture and look at Miguel. "You don't actually have to," I offer. "Your lungs absorb the THC almost instantly."

"I know," says Miguel, releasing the hit with a sudden fierce cough. "But I like to do things the old-fashioned way."

"Well!" My grandmother says. "Well!"

I watch her, waiting for some recrimination.

"This certainly is a lively group! Hipsters without hips. Whaddayou say?"

"You okay, Grandma? You okay with all this? It's for pain, you know."

"I wasn't born yesterday, cookie."

"I'm okay, you're okay—we're all okay," says Claire. "For chrissake."

Miguel takes another toke and passes the joint to Winnie. She giggles, then takes a dainty hit that she coughs out almost at once.

"Don't go wasting that smoke now," says Claire sternly.

Winnie tries and manages to hold it in this time.

Claire grabs the joint and sucks it deeply. She holds her breath longer than she probably should, then releases the smoke in a long, slow thread through her nose and mouth. She takes another quick hit, this time making smoke rings through what seems to be a half-smile. She closes her eyes.

"Whatever happened to smoking?" she asks no one in particular. "Oh, yes, I remember: *It kills.* But it's so wonderful and languid and European. I think…you know what I think? I think that if your kid is killed in a stupid war, then you should be allowed to smoke wherever you damn well want. In restaurants and movie theaters and buses. You should be allowed—just because they've killed your kid."

Anthony reaches across the table and puts his hand on Claire's. "Goddamned right you are! Bastards!"

Everyone is silent, then Claire bursts out laughing. "Goddamn bastards!"

"Bastards!" Anthony roars, laughing so hard that tears come to his eyes. "The bastards," he says in his best Richard Nixon imitation, which gives everyone a new fit of giggles.

"Me next! Me next!" says Selma, and Winnie passes the joint to her.

As Selma inhales, she sways a little back and forth, smiling, then laughs at the punchline of some private joke.

Selma passes the joint to me, and Miguel produces a new one. He's singing out loud, as Anthony hums a completely different tune. My grandmother has the joint now, looking a bit too expert in her inhalation and her heavy-lidded smile.

Miguel gently pulls the joint from Grandma's fingers. "I don't remember the *mota* being this good in my day," he says. "Maybe that's why I went straight to heroin. It was quite wonderful for a while. I used to make these very phallic metal sculptures when I did heroin. Lovely high. Not for the long run, though. Definitely not something for the long run."

Claire snorts a laugh, "Oooh, does anyone remember those little diet pills all the doctors were giving out in the early seventies? They were fun. I got very thin, but very cranky."

"You, dear lady? Cranky?" Anthony chides. "I would never have imagined!"

"Oh, you bastard!" Claire giggles.

"Yes! I remember, yes!" Winnie squeals. "What'd you call them? They were…amphetamines! Gave them out like aspirin. Dr. Levinson…he was very foxy with his chipped front tooth and mutton chops down to here!" Winnie points to either side of her jaw. She's dumped the remainder of Claire's cough drops onto the table and has been arranging them like a string of pearls, though Claire doesn't seem to mind. "We need a needle and thread to make a necklace," Claire says happily.

"Does anyone want to know what I used to do for a living?" my grandmother asks.

I start thinking about pots of rouge and the story she told me when I was a kid about how she once worked for Charles Revson. He founded Revlon, she'd explained. I asked her what Revlon was. "It made ladies beautiful," Grandma replied.

"I want to know, lovely lady," Anthony says.

"You must close your eyes and imagine," Grandma says. "I…was…an escort. I was a knockout, like…Bess…Bess… Bess Mess, poor gal. Bess…Myerson! At the Stage Door Canteen in Manhattan. It was very clean, and the men were very polite…especially Tyrone Power Jr. I was only supposed to be a hostess—you know, dance with the servicemen, have a drink with them, work the coatroom. But then I took Tyrone Power's jacket, and he asked me out—he didn't know I was only fifteen. Mostly they weren't famous, the men. It was fun. Then I stopped—because, you know, the war stopped." She giggles. "One can't do that…forever." Then Selma giggles, and Anthony tips his head to one side, looking like he's in love.

I have no clue who this woman is. She looks like my grandmother and smells like my grandmother, but I can't stop the picture taking shape in my head, of Grandma on her back in her pink cardigan and orthopedic Rockports with her legs and arms spread wide. Oh, man, I can't stop it from coming into focus—a black and white Polaroid of Grandma on her back, her breasts in a puddle on either side of her body, and some movie star standing over her.

"Whoa-wow!" I blurt in an effort to clear the image from my head. "Hooo-man, that's strong stuff, all right."

Grandma catches my eye and frowns. "Oh, shh—it," she says. "Ruthie told me not to tell you that story—oh, damn. You won't tell her I told you, cookie, will you? She thought it'd upset you. But you're not upset—"

"Oh, for Gods sake!" Winnie squeals, before I can even begin to figure out how my mother could've kept that story to herself. "My older sister worked at the Stage Door, too! End of the war—1944. Isn't that something? She only took coats, though."

"My mother was on a boat coming here in 1944. Pregnant with me," Selma says.

"I took a boat ride once," Claire offers. "Never again. Remember all those stupid seniors on that lake upstate in New York not wearing their life preservers? Boat capsizes because they all want to be together, and so they drown together. Not me."

"My cousins stayed in Poland," Selma says. "And so they were killed. *That* was awful."

"Awful," Claire agrees. "Just awful."

There's a lull in the conversation, as everyone seriously ponders just how awful this last awful thing is. No one asks questions or offers to elaborate—probably because they're each taking a moment to recall some awful memory of their own. I've been around them before when this happens. One of them will remember something bad or sad, and then they'll all take a moment or two to silently relive something that was personally sad or terrible long ago, and then—perhaps because they're too close to the *other* end of this journey—they'll continue on with their conversation as if nothing happened. If I asked questions, they'd just realize that I'm not one of them. My cover would be blown—they'd all know I'm not really eighty. My hands…my hands give me away. They're still plump around the knuckles. If I sit on them, no one will notice. Plus I can make my neck and chin look old if I just turn it at the right, weird angle…

"You know what would be awful?" says Selma. "Having someone pull out the stops to keep me alive when it's time to go. That would be awful."

"Hear, hear," says Anthony, taking another toke. Then he hands it to Claire, who says: "Selma, I promise I won't pull out the stops to keep you alive."

"Thank you, Claire."

"And you can just kill me with an elephant gun before I even get to the hospital," Claire continues. "Remember when I was in there for my hip? This little bugger of a nurse says to me, 'How we doing, honey? We taking our meds like a good girl?' And I said to him, '*We're* doing goddamned fine, little boy. Did we take our vitamins today?' That stopped him. That sure as hell stopped him cold."

"I'll bet it did," says Selma with a laugh. "No wonder the poor boy looked scared to death when I came to pick you up."

"Well, speaking of hospitals...Abbie!"

"Claire?" I say, and wait for whatever particular rant Claire has in store.

"Abbie, I've decided to donate my brain for neurological study, to that school you're going to attend—"

"Stanford," Selma offers.

"Uh, I don't even know if I'm taking the scholar—"

"Oh, you're gonna take it, dear," Anthony says, looking at me kindly. "You said it's what you've always wanted. Although Lord knows why a young gal like yourself would want to see a bunch of naked old farts on a regular basis."

"Anthony!" Selma squeals. "Don't scare the girl."

"He doesn't scare me."

"Yeah, Stanford," says Claire. "I want to donate it in your name. Can I do that? I mean, you can donate money or a car in someone's name—I imagine with the right paperwork, you can donate a brain."

I'm floored. "That's—so thoughtful of you, Claire. I read

that they're really short on brain donations. They need normal brains and ones with Alzhei—uh, um," I try to think of how to cover. "And other kinds of brains, you know, for comparison…"

"Well, don't let it get around," she says, without skipping a beat. "I don't want anyone bugging me for my other parts. Just my brain."

"That should keep them busy for a while," Winnie says.

"Maybe you'll have the chance to work on it while you're still there. Not that I plan on going anytime soon—but one never knows."

Another brief lull as we contemplate the fact that no one ever really knows.

"The end is…very messy. Not like, oh, that beautiful woman…Greta," says Grandma.

"Greta Garbo in *Camille*," Claire offers.

"Yes! Beautiful, sad death. I'd go right now, if I had my…druthers. Now. Right now. In this moment. This… perfect day. It's a perfect moment."

Grandma looks off and becomes so still that she seems to have stopped breathing. She is far, far away in a place with no tears and no tomorrows. It's as though she's realized that gravity no longer exists and there's nothing left to hold her to the planet. My hand jerks out from under my leg to grab her arm, catch her, pull her back to our spaceship before she's vaporized by the moonlight, but it doesn't reach and I'm left looking at my outstretched palm.

"It's…it's like…I'm in a jacket," Grandma says, "a white …those jackets that keep crazy people…a straightjacket. I'm in a straightjacket—no, a rubber jacket…a diving suit, with goggles and plugs in my ears…only…only I'm on land. It's…it's so…It's so *frustrating*. I feel…I feel…done. I'm done," she says, turning to me with a slight, faraway smile.

It's Winnie, though, who is able to take her hand and answer her. "I know, hon," she says. "I know exactly what you mean."

"You do. I knew you would. I knew I was here for a reason," my grandmother says quite clearly. And, just as clearly, I know that her reason is not at all the one I had in mind.

⚘   ⚘   ⚘

Folding my outstretched hand after what seems like an hour, I ask, "Miguel, how are you doing?"

"How am I doing? Well, Señorita Abbie, it's my fifth month of hospice and I still won't die. Nobody knows why. Something else is going on—something else is keeping me here, *entienda*? Something bigger. You know what I think it is? What's keeping my blood flowing and my mind intact?"

I lean in and hold my breath. Here it comes, the secret of spiritual awakening…*shaktipat*, baptism, the thing that will swell my senses and swallow my worries, give me game advantage and erase every betrayal that my mother ever inflicted. Seriously, I have been one patient girl, and now my patience is paying off.

I can feel Miguel's breath on my ear as he says it. "I've just finished Sidney Sheldon's eleventh novel, *The Stars Shine Down*. I started reading him when they sent me home. I plan to read them all before I die. All eighteen novels— can you believe that? The man wrote eighteen novels, if you don't count his autobiography. And I plan on finishing them all."

I take the joint that Miguel is offering me and lean back. *Sidney Sheldon*? My brain reels. That must be code, right? And if I break the code I'll learn the meaning of life. Right? Sidney Sheldon…meaning of life…Sidney Sheldon… meaning of life… Then I remember that my mother used to have an old tattered copy of *The Other Side of Midnight* on her bookshelf, nearly swallowed up between two giant encyclopedias.

"Where'd you get this?" I'd asked her. At first she looked confused, almost as though she was seeing it for the first time, as if it had crawled up there and found refuge on her custom-made mahogany shelves. Then a slight smile crept across her face.

"A friend," she said. "An old friend gave it to me."

"Who?"

"A swimmer. She liked the steamy sex parts."

Then the book went away, never to be seen again.

"So I won't die until Mr. Sheldon is finished with me—that much I know," I hear Miguel say with finality.

Across the room, I see that Grandma has been bookended by Anthony and Winnie. They've both taken one of her hands in their own, holding as tightly as I remember my mother holding my hand when I was a small child trying to run out into the crashing waves at the beach. Funny to remember that grasp. Funnier still to see Anthony and Winnie holding Grandma's hands in that way now, and talking to her in low, urgent tones. They're not whispering, yet their voices don't carry to me, not in a way that I can decipher. Oh my God, that's it, they're *encrypting* their conversation. Minutes pass, maybe an hour, but I don't take my eyes off them. And now it's paying off, my vigilance…I start to decode their secret speak.

"We'll take care of it. We can do that." Winnie is saying, patting Grandma's good hand. "Abbie will…" And then they look over at me. Oh, no, they're doing that encryption thing again. Abbie will…Abbie will…Abbie will *what*? Tell me.

Tell me what Abbie will do.

eleven

RUTH

arry has deposited the white paper takeout bags on the kitchen counter and now he's sprawled on the couch, his shoes neatly placed side by side underneath, his eyes closed, his suit jacket pulled tautly around his body to keep it from creasing. I know he's thinking about what we should do next, but I want him to be moving, pacing, doing something to create at least the illusion of furious motion. That's what he's always done in the past, so as to assure me that he's taking care of business, that he has everything under control. And now he's lying still, and I don't like it. It gives the impression of being...finished. And I'm not finished.

"Ruth, sit down. Come here and sit." Harry doesn't even open his eyes as I go to him and sit on the edge of the couch. Slowly and gently, he takes my hand. He's taken my hand like this several times before—when we were waiting to hear whether *Mary Lou and Me* would have a life, visiting me after Abbie was born, when Justin left me, and when I first heard the news of my mother's diagnosis—but something feels different in this gesture now. He holds my cupped hand without speaking. I watch his chest rise, his tie still centered over his shirt buttons, barely askew, his jacket slipped open just enough to reveal the perspiration stains under his armpits. He's taking long, slow breaths. I used to tease him that he followed me out here to California because he couldn't live without me. Big ha ha—that the only reason he took the very prestigious and lucrative job of running the West Coast division of his agency was to look after me, *his first big fish*, as he used to refer to me. "Yeah, baby, that's it," he'd say, smiling. "It was so hard leaving that crappy weather and shoebox apartment to become Big King Shit of the World." I'd smile back, knowing that the truth was somewhere in between. For a moment I wonder what it would be like—so very long after the last time we were together *that* way—to drape myself over his body, unbutton his shirt, and lay my hands over his shoulders with my cheek against his chest. I've had the impulse to kiss Harry exactly twice since the days of our fling: first when *Girls' Guide to New Humans* was published, and then when *Women's Guide to the New Aliens Among Us* came out—probably because good news always weakens my constitution, and one margarita can still make me horny as hell. But I was married the first time and not having sex at all the second (during my year-long experiment with abstinence). And Harry has long since come to consider me family, which makes for an immediate turnoff.

He still hasn't moved. Oddly, I find myself trying to imagine what his obituary would read like—which also kills any last, lingering impulse to do anything more than sit by his side and stare at his perspiration stains. Then my cell phone rings, and Harry lets go of my hand. I leave him to answer my phone in the kitchen.

"Hello, Justin."

"Is this Ruth?"

"Justin, why do you always have to do that—ask whether it's me? Who else would be answering my own cell phone?"

"*Ruth*," says Justin sharply.

"Ugh, God—forget it. I'm sorry, I'm just…"

We both fall silent. I can feel him trying not to channel old, familiar annoyances reserved especially for me, and he can feel that I'm trying—with great difficulty—to keep this civilized. I pace the living room, watching my feet, making sure that I step within the lines of the square tiles. *Step on a crack, break your mother's back.* It's embarrassing for both of us, this silence. Do over. T.O. Time out. I used to say that to him. Then we would both start over. It seemed an amusing routine when we were first together, a funny, breezy way to prevent an argument from becoming a downward spiral, but the intensity of the arguments eventually obliterated that childish gimmick. *Time out*—I'll just say it to myself, in my head. I'll wait. Maybe he'll hear me thinking it. But I don't think he does.

"Justin, um, I'm an idiot," I finally say. "You know—actually, not really. Um…"

"I'll see what I can do, Ruth," Justin says simply. Then he hangs up.

There are two hundred seventy-six comments on yesterday's post and one hundred forty-seven unread messages in my email inbox. They are mostly well meaning and supportive: from women who have a mother or daughter or sister or best friend whom my daughter or my mother remind them of in some *uncanny* way. They offer their sympathy and stories of similar experiences. *Wish you well…hope your mother is in peace…hoping you're able to find the strength to go on…looking forward to your next project…looking forward to hearing your insights on this whole ordeal.* I love these women—love them in a strange and, one might say, codependent way, though I'm loathe to use that term. I mean, if you're human, you're codependent to one degree or another, which means that *admitting* to codependency is a little like declaring that you need to breathe or drink water on a regular basis.

But here they are, the ramblings of four hundred and twenty-three—now four hundred and twenty-four—codependent sisters. And, yes, as long as they don't want more than I can give them, I will love them back.

twelve

ABBIE

It's morning.

I've never slept overnight on the couch before. Turns out it's really uncomfortable and probably more so because I had cottonmouth all night thanks to Miguel's purple pot. I kept waking up for a drink of water, and then I'd check on my grandmother to see whether she was still breathing. And she was, each of the five times I put my ear to her mouth. So I think it's safe to lay here with my eyes closed for a little longer. If I keep completely still and don't breathe, I can even imagine that my grandmother is making me a parsley omelet and has emptied half a box of Skittles into my lunch box, even though I'm not supposed to have them because of my braces. If I keep depriving my body of oxygen, I can actually remember how my legs felt at eight, and how weightless and powerful I felt at that age. Not that I'm fat now, but I just *feel* so much heavier. My head is the heaviest part of me. It's been that way for a long time now.

"Ooooh! Hello?! Where am I?" Grandma's awake. I take a deep breath and come back into my present body. This morning I have more information than I had before, and my grandmother has less. Maybe my grandmother is transferring her memory disc to me but hasn't kept a copy for herself.

"I'm here, Grandma. It's Abbie—you're at my house! I'm here in the living room. I'm coming." But I don't want to move.

"Ooooh, Abbie? That you? I have to pee!"

I'm up.

I wait outside the bathroom door as Grandma's symphony of flatulence continues on without rests. At least she can still pee on her own. I don't know when that will change. I remember the days when Grandma would wipe my behind. "Grandmaaaa! Wipe my bu-uut!" I'd sing from my toilet throne. "Wiiipe my-y bu-utt!" And the amazing thing is that she would, because she was the one around to do it when my mother was working. So it should be that easy, whenever my grandmother reaches that point, for her to simply call out: "Ab—beeeee! Wipe my bu—utt!" And then she'll lean forward, her head pressing against the top of her knees and I'll reach around and do it. But she's a tall woman, Grandma—I won't be able to see what I'm doing, or know how to ask whether she's mortified at my wielding the toilet paper after all these years. Stop it,

Abbie. Stop worrying.

"Gram? Everything okay in there?"

"Everything's okay, sweetie. Your old Grandma still knows how to wipe her own ass." Now she's reading my mind. "You need to keep some baby oil in here, where I can reach."

"Okay." I don't want to know why she needs baby oil near the toilet. "I'll go shopping today."

"Then we ought to call your mother." A minute passes while I think how to answer this. "Then I'll drive you to school. You've probably missed your bus."

"Grandma? You're at my house in the desert. Winnie is coming by for lunch. Remember Winnie?"

Grandma is silent for a few seconds. "I know that, honey…I just wanted to see…if you were listening. Now go away. I'll be right out."

🖱 🖱 🖱

Twenty minutes later, Grandma and I are in the kitchen and I'm making a pomegranate spritzer. "You'll love this, seriously," I tell her.

"You know," she starts, smiling slyly, "Miguel is in love with Winnie. And that hard-boiled birdie, Claire, she would like to sleep with Anthony."

"Oh, God, Grandma, you're not serious about Claire. *God*, Grandma."

"*God*, Abbie," Grandma says, mockingly. "Don't be embarrassed. It's just the truth."

"I'm not. I'm not embarrassed. Grandma, do you remember something you said last night…about—the Stage

Door Canteen?"

Grandma stares out the window, shaking her head. "I had a long life before I met you, cookie. Never make excuses for your life."

"I know, I was just surprised—"

"I have an itch over my ear. I can't reach it. I think I may be shrinking."

She can't reach it because she can't move her arm. "It's the damnedest thing," she continues, "everything shrinking except my nose. It's embarrassing. You know nothing ever embarrassed your mother. Nothing that I know of. How a person, a girl, can not be embarrassed by anything. I think that's a great…acc—accom, um, *ac-com-plish-ment*, don't you?"

"Um, I don't know how great that is, Grandma. It could just mean that she's missing some human quality, you know? I mean, there's no arguing with Ruth, because it's like she doesn't *understand* if you disagree with her. I mean, you don't argue with an autistic person, and Ruth is, like, *autistic* when it comes to arguments. I'm sorry, Grandma—does this make any sense?"

"So, you think…you think…the Guru-gundas will not think well of her?"

Before she can finish, my grandmother knows that she's left for a moment—once again let go again of the rope mooring her to the mothership, floated away momentarily, and rode back on an asteroid. She doesn't remember her trip but knows she's taken one, because she wrinkles her brow in fleeting confusion. She recovers in an instant, though. "May you have a long life with no embarrassment," she says. "Or excuses."

"What do you mean?"

"Your mother is a sensitive girl. Too much anxiety for one girl. Where did that come from?"

Grandma's lost in space, again.

"Where…does…it…origin?" And she winces, this time from a pain in her belly. "Oh!"

"I have something for you, Grandma. Wait a minute!" I search in my knapsack for a sheet of pills—each in their own little indented plastic compartment with a foil cover—labeled "Esther Sternberg. For pain. Morphine." If I were five, I'd ask my grandmother to save the sheet so I could put a Tic Tac in each tiny rectangular compartment. I don't know how I could be such a tool, but I somehow interpreted "For pain" to mean "For pain only if you feel pain, and you probably won't feel pain for a while." I don't know what I was thinking. Why would I think that "For pain" meant for pain sometime in the far-off future? I peel back the foil on one of the pills and hand it to her with the spritzer. She dribbles the dark liquid down her chin and swallows hard several times before she's able to speak again.

"Thank you, *darling*."

Darling? I have never been "darling." I've been "cookie" and "sweetheart" and "honey" and "Miss Smartypants," but never "darling."

"You are you, is who," Grandma answers, reading my mind again. "Just like Doctor Seuss. Yes, just like that. Now if you just help me with my shirt, I can do the rest. Time to get dressed, yes?"

I do as Grandma asks, helping her back to the bedroom

and into a beige blouse, buttoning each tiny plastic flower-
button, then pulling a skirt over her head and down to
her waist. I take a hairbrush off the dresser, but Grandma
waves me off, patting her brown-dyed hair—which is on
its fourth day from a beauty-parlor visit—into place. "You
go. I'll join you in a minute."

Winnie cries, "Halloo!" as she sails through the back
door. I hallooo back. She sets the bags of arugula and tiny
squash from her garden and the brown bag of store-bought
stuff on my counter, then starts putting it all away. I sit
and watch her moving efficiently through my kitchen,
humming to herself, grabbing old food from my fridge and
checking the dates, then tossing out most of it. She wears
a tight bun at the nape of her neck and a powder-blue,
sleeveless turtleneck. Winnie used to be a skier. Alpine.
Her home is filled with photographs of her standing around
with other skiers, sitting in rustic lodges with friends. The
photographs are all framed and older than I am, but she
can tell you the names of every person in them, as well as
who snapped the picture and who wiped out on the hill
that day. She met her husband on a hill, picked him up
from a face-down wipeout that knocked off a ski and left
him with a minor concussion. He claimed to have seen
two Winnies the moment she appeared by his side. He
said later that he'd finally seen the woman he was going to
marry and, damn, she was twins! Winnie's version is that
he took the spill just to meet ladies that weekend. They
laughed every time they told the story together, she told
me, laughed untill he died and there was no one to do his
side of the routine. Winnie still wears her turtlenecks, even

in summer. She lived in them skiing and thought they were more flattering than any other shirt style. So she has them in silk, cotton, and wool, with sleeves and without, ribbed, rolled, and knit. Pale blue is also her color: It sets off her blue eyes and makes her silver hair seem iridescent.

Winnie finishes putting the groceries away and starts a pot of tea as Grandma teeters into the room. Winnie hugs her, then leads her to a chair. I can see Grandma's got on a smidge of too-red lipstick. It looks like a short, red horizontal pipe cleaner below her nose, her lips too thin and inward-turning to bear the weight of the color. She's also added a black cashmere cardigan over her shoulders, over the beige blouse. She whispers something to Winnie, and they both smile at me.

"Well, we should call...Ruth!" Grandma says suddenly. "Shouldn't we?"

"Grandma," I say as casually as possible, "uh, I—I'm sorry I didn't wake you when Ruth called last night, but, I meant to tell you. Anyway, Mom did call already."

"Oh! That's too bad I missed her."

"Yeah, well...see, she asked me to apologize to you, and to say that she was going to take the next couple of days to work on something, since I told her we were having such a good time and all. So...we won't be able to reach her—you know how she won't answer the phone if she's working. I guess we'll just have to wait."

"Oh, I understand. Do you know what she's...um, writing?"

"Uh, nope."

"A nnn...nov...a book. Another book. That would

make her very happy. We'll be sure and ask."

"Caffeine or no caffeine?" Winnie interjects.

"Is there any of that…marijuana left?" Grandma says.

"Are you serious?" I ask her, and the two of them burst out laughing—at me. I wonder whether it might be a good idea to keep Grandma stoned for the duration—at least until I'm arrested, or until my mother finds and kills me.

"Okay," I say, "now you're sure about this afternoon? I wasn't supposed to work, but it's only a half a shift, until Meg gets there…"

"Don't worry," Winnie says. "We'll be fine. We'll be right here. We're not going to get rowdy while you're gone," she laughs.

"All right. I'm just going to make a quick call, then I'm leaving."

I step into the bedroom, close the door, and pick up the receiver of the dusty, neglected landline that came with the cottage. I dial my father, who picks up on, like, the seventeenth ring. We small talk until I bring up "the thing."

"Thanks, Justin, for not telling Ruth."

He's known my plans all along. He didn't necessarily approve of any of it, just like he never approved of my calling him "Justin" instead of "Dad," or of my putting off college to spend some time by myself in a dusty Arizona town. But he would never actually express his disapproval, because, as he's fond of pointing out in such cases, it's his problem, not mine. "Grandma is fine," I tell him. "She's okay."

"Have you given any thought to—"

"I have too many thoughts as it is, so I decided I'm just going to ignore them all," I cut in, beating him to the punch.

"Maybe I should start up a website, something catchy like Ruth-Sternberg-Is-an-Opportunistic-Prehistoric-Predator-dot-com?" Justin doesn't react.

"Why don't you let me help?" he says after a moment.

"Help me do what?"

He is silent. Neither of us know what that help would look like exactly. I know he's frowning, the dimpled worry lines reaching into the crown of his tan, bald head. Justin has been bald and frowning at the idiocy of loved ones ever since I can remember. My best friend Izzie called him Daddy Warbucks until she was nearly thirteen, then gave that up for Grandmaster Zenbo, because of my father's extreme patience. His patience with me, patience with my boy-crazy friends, patience—at first—with my crazy celebrity mother and the psychos who spilled out of the woodwork asking her to speak at functions, dinners, openings, commencements, and funerals, patience with the women who swarmed his yoga class every morning at eight. The yoga and bodywork stuff didn't come until long after his master's degree in literature and minor in Eastern philosophy, until after a single, failed novel and his attempts to see the literary light from under a total eclipse by my mother. The fact is that Justin is an inspired yoga teacher and an excellent ridder of excess angst through craniosacral bodywork—seriously, that's what he does. His clients say he's a magician.

"Ruth Sternberg is bright and charming and infuriating," is what my father said about my mother when they first met, when he interviewed the then-twenty-one-year-old author for his college paper. She was high on double espressos and Camel Lights, and loud enough to be heard over the roar of the school's dining hall. He was the paper's editor-in-chief, hung over and none too happy about being called in to pinch-hit on an interview with some spoiled girl writer. Back in those days, my mother—or so my father's side of the story goes—was beguiling, obnoxious, and beautiful, and she looked at him as though she might climb him naked at any moment and pirouette on the top of his head. About Justin, my mother claimed that she'd never wanted anything in her life—aside from recognition— more than him…probably because he was one of the few people she'd met who didn't want her in the same way at first. Both of them insist that it was terrific and crazy in the beginning, that they couldn't rip their clothes off fast enough, that they lived in each other's back pockets and absolutely needed to share their every thought. Eventually, all that passion was distilled down to some toxic brew of disappointment and recrimination, the exact recipe for which neither wants to remember.

My father loves me and wants to help; I know that. And the truly strange thing is that I'm pretty sure Justin has never stopped loving my mother, either. But I think he'd sooner be seen eating a Big Mac or punching Buddha in the face than actually admit to that.

thirteen

RUTH

H arry, how do we know for sure this is the right address?"
Harry continues to drive, looking straight ahead behind his aviators, pretending to be deep in thought. I'm
sure he's trying to determine how exactly we'll approach
my lovely daughter without bodily or professional harm
coming to either of us, but he's also worrying about missing
two capoeira classes at his gym, as well as his weekly
manicure, and how he'll explain his favoritism toward
me to Lydia—sexy, young, Iowa Writers Workshop Lydia
with the Next Important Novel in her appropriately ratty
vintage cycle bag, whom he's just signed because her book
will make a great *film*. Lydia's posture alone, the way she
oh-so-negligently tosses back her corn-silk hair, says: "Oh,
Harry, I don't need anything but this grungy, perfectly
aged leather motorcycle bag to tote around my already-
much-heralded first novel that I began in between stints in

the Peace Corps and getting my master's in sociology." Oh, *please*. Harry's actually said that Lydia's too intellectual for his tastes. So what does that say about me?

"Harry. Harry! Can you answer me? Your nails look fine."

"What? Ruth, what are you talking about?"

"Nothing. Who did you get Abbie's address from?"

"It's too long a story. I'm too tired."

"I hate the desert," I say after a moment. "Why does everyone say that desert air is so transforming? It makes my skin feel like parchment! You want rejuvenation, you have to go to San Francisco—or Long Island, God forbid—and find some humidity."

We're on our way to Burbank Airport, where we'll board a commuter plane to Phoenix, then drive to Tucson. I also hate commuter planes—everyone on them looks dressed for sudden death. A group of business travelers in tasteful suits and nice shoes: *Hello, I'm already dressed for my coffin, so please don't worry if you crash and kill me.* Jesus Christ, I hate these flights.

"Los Angeles is a desert, Ruth," Harry reminds me. "And you live here."

True enough. That wasn't always the case, but it sure does seem that way sometimes. It's been twenty years since I lived anywhere else, and then it was always within a forty-mile radius of Manhattan's Midtown Tunnel. Sometimes I can't remember how Justin and I got here, because I've put a comic gloss on the details of our trip a few too many times in too many articles, and that seems to have erased most of the actual memories. We were only planning to visit, a couple of months at most—to watch them film the movie version of *Mary Lou and Me*, meet its star, Winona Ryder, take the tour at Universal Studios, and witness the parting of the Red Sea. There are photos of that trip, of me standing awkwardly beside a grazing cow or next to the barbed wire of a roadside chicken farm or in front of a concrete-block motel with tumbleweeds caught in blurred motion in the foreground. I think I touched Justin all the way here. These days, all I remember of that trip is what I've written about it since then, and what was captured in those photographs. Everything else ended up in parentheses, and I haven't revisited those details in years. I know that it was winter, and I was in corduroys and a thermal top as we drove past a sign welcoming us to Los Angeles. It was at dusk, the sky an altogether different hue of orange and red than is possible anywhere on the East Coast.

We finally pulled into a coffee shop on Sunset Boulevard near Cahuenga, where girls sat in booths in halter tops and sandals—in January—the kind of girls I imagined would be working as extras on the movie of *Mary Lou and Me*. The menu boasted every type of burger except vegetarian— which surprised me, because I'd seen *Annie Hall* one too many times—and with every kind of topping under the sun. I went with the Metamorphism Turkey Burger, because it promised to change my outlook on life by virtue of its topping of cherries, blue cheese, and grilled endive. Justin ordered the Karma and Cheese (macaroni in a pesto cheese sauce with bacon bits). We wound up spending most of that night in the emergency room of Children's Hospital, where I was treated for a severe case of food poisoning. Justin decided it was a sign that we needed to turn around first thing in the morning, head back to the East Coast, and kick the subletter out of our lower-Manhattan place. But I convinced him otherwise—because of the dream I had after nodding off in the waiting room.

I'd been reading an article in the *L.A. Times*—in between bouts of dry-heaving into a plastic bowl—about a promising young writer who had died in a plane crash en route to the set where his first-ever screenplay was being shot as a big-budget Hollywood movie. I read that he'd crashed in one of those single-engine death traps made infamous by Patsy Cline and Buddy Holly. The article said that his last telephone call on the ground had been to his girlfriend, forgiving her for some tawdry affair with his best friend; his second-to-last phone call was to that friend, forgiving *him*. Then he'd boarded that single-engine plane and crashed, without fog or instrument failure or pilot error, back into the runway right upon takeoff. In my dream, I stood watching from the tarmac as my best friend Missy was wheeled on a stretcher to the small plane's boarding ladder. I knew that Missy was paralyzed under the white sheets, but only her head and face were visible. I moved closer, excited to see her, because it had been years since the accident in Andy Levy's pool—when Missy dove into the not-quite-deep-enough end and, within an instant, severed all communication between her brain and limbs. Forever paralyzed, everyone said. And since her family moved away without so much as a "goodbye" shortly after the accident, it happened to be forever before I'd see her again.

In my dream, Missy was weeping. She turned her head and cried to me that she couldn't walk up the steps so I must go *for* her—take her seat on the flight. "Go," she said, "take the trip because *you* can." And in that dream—a dream that's never failed to recur in the most anxiety-filled times of my life—I got on the plane. I took my seat on that fucking single-engine plane and I took that trip for Missy.

I woke from that dream—that first time I had it, in that hospital waiting room—with newsprint on my cheek and a headache that threatened to blow a hole through my right temple. What I suddenly knew was that I had to take a chance—I had to trust the trip ahead. Then I puked onto the newspaper.

🖰　🖰　🖰

"Freeze and La Prairie are interested in the site for their new creams. Did I tell you that?" Harry says to me as we near the airport. I know him well enough to know that he's trying to distract me, so I'd forget all about that commuter flight out of Burbank that crashed into Catalina Island last month.

"Great," I say. "What does that mean? They think I attract rich mommies with wrinkles?"

"You use the stuff," he says, annoyed.

"So?"

"Just be impossible, Ruth. Go ahead."

I would if I had the energy; instead I think of my own skin and the skin on the women who read my blog and write to me and comment daily. "*That woman* wrote to me again," I tell Harry. "The one I told you about, who sounds—I don't know—*familiar.* Just her tone, like she knows me—"

"They all know you," he deadpans.

"No, there's something off about her. She doesn't have the same vibe as the others. It's…she's…

"Another crazy mother from your deep, dark past…"

"You're a crazy mutha, Harry. This one doesn't have kids, okay? She told me so."

"Then she's probably just one of those eccentric cat ladies," Harry says, bored with the conversation. "But don't hold it against her." Weirdly, I seem to detect a certain cautionary note in his voice, as if Harry secretly thinks that I'm well on my way to becoming one of those eccentric cat ladies myself. I don't have time to retaliate because we abruptly pull into the vortex that is the Burbank Airport parking lot, near the tarmac that, remarkably, resembles the one in my dream.

fourteen

ABBIE

I like being at work. It's kind of Zenlike sometimes; chop wood, carry double cappuccinos. Today I wasn't scheduled to come in, but I'll only be here a few hours, because the boss is having a root canal and she can't leave Leo in charge—twenty-two-year-old Leo, who thinks that Minecraft is the greatest technological achievement of the twenty-first century. So far I've polished the espresso machine, cleaned the upchuck from a little kid who vomited chocolate croissants on the diaper station, and re-made three of Leo's lame frappes.

Leo's laughing out loud. "You have to see this. It's so funny!"

Leo's on a Vine binge. He's been here two and a half hours and done, like, twenty-two minutes of work, which means that—since each video is really closer to six *and a half* seconds, not six—he's watched like eleven thousand videos. I don't know why, but watching too many of those things in a row makes me feel like I have the flu.

"Leo. Leo!"

"What? What's wrong?" he says, yanking his ear buds out by the cords.

"You have to check the men's room. Have you done that?"

He looks confused, like he's just materialized from another century. "Leo. The. Men's. Room?"

"Yeah, yeah, sorry." He cocks his head, aware of the music. "What are we listening to?"

"It's Marvin Gaye."

"You like this stuff?"

"It's classic."

"Uh-huh. It's like that la-la-la stuff, singing about a picnic basket."

"Ella Fitzgerald. Tisket a tasket. And it's a completely different era."

"Allofit who?"

"Leo. Your total lack of gravitas is awe-inspiring. Really, I mean it."

His eyes widen, "Dude," he says solemnly. "Thanks, man. That means a lot coming from you."

"*Dude*, you're welcome."

"Excuse me." Leo and I look up to see an elderly man in a worn but pressed three-piece tweed suit in front of the counter. "I don't mean to interrupt," he says politely.

"Hey, don't look now, but your date's here," Leo whispers to me out the side of his mouth, then disappears behind the Danish display and starts tapping on his phone. "Hi, what can I get for you?"

"Oh, just a coffee, please, in one of those good old porcelain cups," the man says with a very slight German accent. He looks up from under his natty tweed cap, pulled down over long white hair in a ponytail, and smiles. Then he hooks his walking cane on one arm and pays me with his free hand.

I smile back. "First refill is free."

He winks. With his hands on either side of the saucer at three and nine o'clock and his forearms exactly parallel to the floor, to balance the hanging cane, he maneuvers his way to a table. I love this man I've never seen before—love his deliberate dress and manner and the time he takes to move through moments. I want to watch him some more, but he's disappeared around the corner. This is why I don't look at boys my own age—I'm too busy watching their grandfathers. I figure by the time you're eighty-five, chances are no one's left who remembers the person you were at twenty. I mean, who knows: This man could have fled the Nazis, or he could have *been* a Nazi, or he could have spent his whole life happily married to his childhood sweetheart, or had sex with prostitutes on a number of occasions because he hated his wife. How would I feel about him if I knew *that*? And if I were eighty-five and he and I were dating, and he was kind and considerate, would it really matter who he had been at twenty?

"Hello...again!" A guy is calling from the counter. He's in his early twenties, and I recognize him from my last shift: He ordered a caramel macchiatto in a takeout cup (which no one ever does) and paid for it with a twenty, sat at a table for an hour without once texting, then ordered another one. I remember things like that. Also the fact that I almost tripped over his orange-and-black-checkered high-tops when I took my break.

"Caramel macchiatto?"

"You're good," he says. "How did you know?"

"I've only made two all week."

"Both times for me?"

"You got it," I say, turning my back on him to make his drink.

I drop three drips of steamed milk in the shape of a three-leaf clover over the caramel-colored liquid. Perfect. He pays and tips me a dollar, then he sits at a table and takes out his phone, which reminds me that I should check in with Winnie.

"Leo, let me borrow your cell." Leo looks panicked, as if he was afraid he won't be able to breathe if his thumbs aren't moving. "Leo." He juts out his lower lip and tosses his phone to me. "Pay attention. Customers. I'll be back in a few."

I grab the last cheese croissant and sit by the window. Before I can dial, though, high-top boy is pulling up a chair. He doesn't sit, just looks at me like he needs something—maybe a signature on a petition to save the giant saguaros. Those guys are always pulling up chairs next to me. They're so earnest and needy, in an amusing way—like they need you to know how seriously they take their time on this planet. They also tend to be wearing a "Save the Something or Other" T-shirt layered over long-sleeved rugby shirts. This one is wearing a red wool ski cap with a pom-pom on top, which he yanks off like a boy might do in one of those old-fashioned gestures of courtesy when meeting his girlfriend's parents for the first time. The dry room static holds a few long strands of his thick, matted hair skyward. He's...beautiful, I think, in a way that always makes me uneasy. Boys with his kind of bones usually greet girls my age with "Whoa!" and "Dude!" and get blushes in return. He swallows hard and says *my name*.

"I'm sorry, how do I know you?" I say, warily. His knee-length board shorts in a yellow hibiscus print fan out from under a Carhartt jacket. He reaches into his knapsack, pulls out an iPad, and places it in front of me like an offering.

"We've never met, really," he says. "My name is Eric. Eric Smith. I...I'm a documentary filmmaker and I've been trying to find you for a while now."

I wish he just had a petition to sign. But no—he's one of those people who occasionally pop up wanting to disseminate the freak show that was my life. Though he doesn't fit the general M.O. of those people—they tend to be middle-aged journalists, professional bloggers, or just fans of my mother. I've found that it's best to be short, polite, and boring with them. "And now you have," I say, in a monotone.

"Uh, I'd like to talk to you...about doing your story. I think the way you're dealing with your life these days speaks to this basic need for privacy and self-respect in... in a world gone crazy with self-promotion and, well, you know—"

"I'm really not interested," I say.

"Um, well, obviously, I figured you'd say that, but I'm

not ready to take no for an answer. If you could just give me a few minutes—I've been camped out here for three days. You didn't come in yesterday," he adds almost accusingly.

This could be headed into weirdness, so I put on my best vacant stare—the one that hints that I could become catatonic at any moment.

"Listen, I'm for real," he continues. "I had a documentary on the Sundance Channel last year. They featured it on Hulu. Maybe you saw it—I followed these uber-talented Chinese twins who play steel guitar. Long story short: Unhappy child prodigies, their immigrant parents wanted them to play classical Chinese music, but they threw it over once they got hooked on American blues…um, they were at Coachella two years ago. Crazy talented…"

"I saw that!" I say, involuntarily snapping out of my zombie gaze. "The Leung twins. They're amazing. They're like Roy Ayres meets the Ahn Trio. You did that?"

"Uh-huh. So you liked it?"

"It was okay," I say, quickly retreating.

"Well, here's what I was thinking…"

"Right, so like I said before, I'm not really interested in having a documentary made on the, um, story of my life. Kinda been there before, know what I'm saying?"

"You'd have as much input…"

"And, anyway, the next couple months aren't really good for me," I say, interrupting him. "It's, um, a complicated situation. But how 'bout this? Why don't you give me your number, and after it's through, I'll give you a call and you can come back here, and then we'll talk. We'll have a good long talk. Okay?"

"Maybe it's something I can help with," says Eric. "I'm especially good with complicated situations."

"Thanks, no—I'm good."

"I'm also really trustworthy. More than most people. I have to be, to do what I do. I have to be, you know..."

"Trustworthy," I say, impatiently.

"Yeah, exactly."

It's weird, as annoying as this is getting, I'm not entirely displeased by Eric's attention. I think I'm a good judge of character, and he seems earnest enough. Maybe not harmless—he's too good-looking to be completely harmless—but earnest.

"I'm sorry, Eric, but I've really got to go."

"Can I show you something very personal?"

"No. No, don't show me anything, please."

"It'll just take a second." And before I can say anything, Eric slips the iPad on the table and gives it a couple taps. There's a voiceover, speaking about *me*, with a rough montage of *photos of my life*.

"After her childhood, Abbie Handler would have preferred to never be in the public consciousness again. That alone would make her an enigma for my generation. In this age of relentless self-hype and personal confession, when everybody wants to be on reality TV and the number of bloggers on the internet rapidly approaches 150 million, Abbie Handler is the last holdout. Six months ago, she left California and, much to the dismay of readers of Full Nest/Life Beyond Motherhood—the long-running, mega-popular blog by Abbie's mother, Ruth Sternberg—she seems to have dropped off the face of the earth. Overnight,

Ruth Sternberg was deprived of her best-known subject—almost as if Holden Caulfield had run out on J.D. Salinger without leaving a forwarding address."

Eric taps the screen. "It's still rough. A little too... dramatic." He laughs. "I don't know. I mean, I'd love to have your input—"

"Wh-what is that?" I say. "That's not okay. Is that for the movie?"

"Documentary," says Eric.

"No, no, you can't do that. It's against the law."

"No, technically it's not, since you're a public figure—"

"Okay," I say, "wait. Be quiet. Lemme think here."

He manages to follow directions, but for only a moment. "Abbie," he says, "I know, I'm totally catching you unawares. I know, because it's sort of how I felt when I first moved to L.A. Like—perfect example: I live near the Observatory, so I started hiking, because that's what people do there, right? And I'm a friendly guy, but not overly so—sometimes I'm a little suspicious of people—but I do this hike, and all these people who I don't know, who are doing the same hike in the opposite direction, say hello, like they know me. I mean, not just hello, but 'Hello, hey, how you doin'?' And at first it caught me completely off guard, but before I knew it, I was saying the same back, because I'd been *disarmed*. You know?"

Disarmed is a pretty good word for how I feel now, but I'm not about to tell him that. There's something about listening to his soft baritone voice—which sounds like one of those whispy storytellers on *This American Life* who make you want to stay parked in your car, listening, like you're eavesdropping on sex. He's having that effect on me, this Eric guy. Or maybe it's because of the way those lips, which seem too wide and soft to support language, are working extra hard to lay out his case. Or no, maybe it's because of that direct—but not menacing—gaze above those lips. Fortunately, I've spent years practicing my poker face, the one I now wear.

"I don't know many people in L.A. yet," he continues after a moment, not sure what kind of progress he's making. "Not *well* anyway. I've been there about a year. I like it, but, I mean, it's not easy to find the city's *center*. You have to make your own center, which feels almost impossible because of the sprawl of the place. Does that make any sense? You really have to work at creating your identity there. I mean, I'm Eric Smith, twenty-five years old; I'm a full-time EMT and a part-time documentary filmmaker whose zip code is 90042...which says what? Right? I mean, in New York, I was a New Yorker and that was enough. That was my identity. That's the identity of most people who live there and it's definitely *enough*. You're a New Yorker—it means you conquer the odds, ride mass transit, and have everyone in your face, and at the end of the day you're a survivor. But in Los Angeles, I mean...is *Los Angeleno* even a real word?"

"Ummm..." I say. But before I can even begin to process any of this, I hear someone else calling my name: "Abbie!"

Miguel is standing in the doorway of the coffee shop, leaning against his walker, calling my name in his crackling, sing-song voice. "Abbie! What's a-cookin'?" Selma stands by his side, a colored pencil behind each ear and an easel under her arm. They both look like they've been blown sideways by the desert winds, and probably have been after spending the early afternoon painting landscapes and, in Selma's case, naked men.

"Yoo-hoo, honey!" she calls.

Eric's attention snaps instantly to them. "Family?" he asks.

Selma lays her easel aside and pulls two chairs up to our table. She and Miguel are positively *beaming* at Eric. "Hello!" Selma gushes.

"Hello there," Eric beams back.

"I'm sorry—I hope we're not interrupting your date," Miguel says slyly.

"No, no!" I say. "No date. Not a date. This is Eric."

"Eric!" says Selma. "Like that lovely man from the art center who died in that fire last year. You remember, Abbie? He was sweet on Winnie, but deaf as a post. Miguel, you remember? Eric, it's nice to meet you."

"Same here," says Eric, shaking her hand. "And you are?"

"I'm Selma, and this is Miguel," says Selma. "Oooh—cold hands, warm heart!"

"So I've been told," says Eric, gallantly. Then, eyeing her easel: "Great light for painting this time of day."

"Yes, but the shadows…" Selma begins.

"The shadows seem so much longer today than yesterday," Miguel puts in.

"How strange—I thought that, too," Selma says, wistfully. "And colder. It was forty-six degrees when I woke up this morning. Four degrees cooler than yesterday. No setting one's watch by *that*," she says, and then points to my croissant. "May I?"

"It's yours," I say, pushing the plate to her.

"Thermometer on the bank said fifty-seven degrees not five minutes ago," Miguel says. "Sixty-four an hour ago when we stopped for gas. It's starting to drop faster now."

"I'll bet we see some record-breakers after this drought," Selma says.

It's funny how they like to talk about the weather, how they almost root for it like bettors at a racetrack—like it's some whimsical friend who can be surprising or menacing or comforting by turns.

Eric chimes in: "Did you know that one of the greatest temperature changes ever recorded happened in a place called Spearfish, South Dakota, in 1943? It went from four degrees below zero to forty-five degrees above in the space of two minutes. That's like a complete climate change in less time than it takes to boil water."

Miguel laughs, shaking his head madly up and down in agreement. "You don't even know it's happening until it's happened!" he says. "Like you're a lobster in a pot!"

"Mmm-mm," Selma says, chewing serenely on a piece of croissant.

"And the worst thing is, there's nothing you can do about it," Miguel adds. "You can't change the weather, and a lot of the time you can't even predict it! It's just one of those things you have to accept."

"Totally," Eric says.

Selma gulps to make room for an answer. "Like life. Or the people we love. Or frien—" But she doesn't finish.

"Fruh! Uh!" Selma coughs, then tries to suck in a breath of air but gasps instead, her eyes bugging open. Gagging, she pushes away from the table and pounds her chest with one fist and raises the other, fingers splayed and stiff.

"Oh my God—she's choking!" I yell. "Oh my God! Selma!"

Before my brain can settle on a plan, Eric moves behind Selma and tightens his arms around her body. He squeezes his fists together just under her breasts and pulls in hard...once, twice, again and again. Selma grunts in little bursts, an engine sputtering out of fuel, then she starts coughing—and after that, breathing. Several customers have surrounded our table and are asking what we need, while I sit, totally useless, the hapless bystander in some instructional video about the Heimlich maneuver, staring stupidly until the hero shows up and sends the chewed food shooting like a projectile out of the victim's mouth. Tragedy averted. Fade out on the protagonist holding up the old woman who is wiping her hand across her mouth, and an old man looking relieved, and a girl staring dumbly, frozen in place. Selma collapses into a chair, and then I thaw out enough to take her hands. "Selma, Selma..."

"I'm...okay," she says, taking a slow breath. "I'm fine."

"She's fine, she's fine," Miguel echoes, stroking the back of her head.

Eric stands apart from us, looking away, pretending to be absorbed in a watercolor on the wall. He smoothes down his hair, clears his throat, but stays silent. Not even a minute passes, but it feels like the whole afternoon, then Selma goes over and hugs him. "Thank you, dear," she says.

"Obviously, the timing was wrong for my demise."

"Timing is everything," Miguel says.

"That was amazing," I mumble—but truthfully, now I want Eric gone even more than before. I'm beyond grateful, which makes me beyond uncomfortable.

I busy myself cleaning up while the three of them make small talk. I give Leo his phone back and tell him I'm leaving, and he doesn't argue with me. He's even managed to find and dispose of the chewed pastry piece that rocketed over the counter, and now he's furiously polishing the display case, staring at Selma and Eric as he pushes the rag. "Fucking awesome!" he says. "I almost had a fucking heart attack. That was like *The Exorcist* meets *Cake Boss*!"

I wait a few minutes before rejoining the group, not quite sure how to break up the party. "Eric." The three of them look up at me. "You—you'll be late. Um, you…thank you, really. I know we've kinda kept you. I know you need to *leave*."

I clench my teeth, breathing through my ears, willing Eric to say his goodbyes and be gone. Widening my eyes, I gesture to the door with my chin, tightening my lip. I probably look like I'm pretending to be a gorilla.

Eric hesitates, then puts his hand on my arm. "Abbie, I can *totally* rearrange my schedule," he says evenly—but I notice that his hand is trembling.

"What a nice boy," Selma says. "And a hero, too."

"Nah, not even," he says. Then he takes his hand off my arm and pushes the small beads of sweat that have formed on his forehead back into his thick black hair. His hair, too long to stay in place, springs haphazardly back onto his pale face, the contrast perfect for a black-and-white photo. If his eyes weren't so animated and his expression so incredibly earnest, he could pass for one of those models wearing a dark Italian suit in some glossy fashion magazine.

"Miguel, are you okay?" I ask.

"I'm good. It's all good."

"Oh, Abbie!" Selma says. "I almost forgot to tell you—he had some of that you-know-what after breakfast. Kept all his food down. Even made him hungry for more."

"That's right," Miguel says. "I was like a starved man eating for the first time."

"We're getting ice cream for tonight. You ought to come too, Eric. Everyone would love to meet you." Then, lowering her voice conspiratorially: "You do smoke marijuana occasionally, don't you?"

"Eric really has to head off," I say, apologetically. "Eric, you really should go. Now. I'll take your number. I *promise* I'll call."

"Is that the way it works now—the boys wait by the phone?" Miguel says.

"I wouldn't mind hanging a bit more," Eric says. "Um, marijuana, yeah, I've been known to burn a little weed in my time," he says to Selma, then pats his jacket pocket meaningfully. "But if you're smoking marijuana medicinally, you really should think about using a vaporizer. A friend of mine in L.A. swears by it. He keeps telling me to try it—"

"How 'bout now. Why don't you *vaporize* right now?" I blurt out.

Selma and Miguel look confused. "Actually, it's a little too early in the day for me," Eric says smoothly. "Besides,

I've always been more of a coffee-bean guy myself."

"My kind of man!" Selma says.

"All right," Miguel says. "We should hit the road, eh?"

"Alrighty then," Eric says brightly.

Alrighty then? I don't believe it. *"Alrighty,"* I say, drawing out the syllables through clenched teeth, but Eric doesn't notice—or if he does, he's pretending not to.

fifteen

RUTH

Harry is asleep in the passenger seat. How considerate that his response to stress is the opposite of mine. I suppose I didn't need that last Super Gulp barrel of coffee. Too late: Harry sleeps so that I don't have to. Maybe that's it. What are we driving anyway? Ah, yes, a Leaf. Harry rented us a fucking Leaf. He's so considerate—could we rent an uglier car? I drive one of these things at home, but that's because I have to, because it's not enough to *care*. I have to *look* like I care, otherwise I might as well drive a Hummer. At least I don't drive a Mini, which just screams fortysomething wanting to appear twentysomething. It's a road trip, though. We ought to be driving a Lincoln, or a diesel Mercedes, or a fucking Buick. Bless Harry for his well-intentioned greenness. He's trying to make up for his twice-daily ten-minute showers—or maybe for having his six-hundred-thread-count sheets laundered as often as his

half-acre of hardly indigenous to Southern California Ken-
tucky bluegrass is watered. Harry means well. He also
loves the desert with the same enthusiasm that I dislike
it, although he loves it wrapped around an infinity-pool
oasis with modern adobe bungalows. He loves the postcard
beauty of the desert from the window of a spa restaurant
serving eight hundred balanced calories of lobster salad.
*Lobsters are not found in the desert, Harry. Shouldn't you eat
cactus flower soufflés and small, roasted prairie animals when
in the desert?*

I do like Joshua trees, though. What is it about them?
They're biblical—they can only survive at a specific altitude
in a certain heat. So ugly and crooked, vulnerable, solitary.
If a Joshua tree was a person, it might be Keith Richards
without the eyeliner. Everything and everyone looks so
much older in the desert.

My hands, my poor, sad hands, never catch a break
from the sun and air—thousands of tiny creases and
cracks from wrists to fingertips, like a decades-dry lake
bed turning to talc. My veins resemble beads threaded on
a crooked cord, only becoming taut and smooth when I
make a fist. The state of my hands, the dry heat of the
car, and the fact that I have no idea what I will say to
my daughter when I find her makes me quite suddenly
and unbearably sleepy. I try opening my eyes as wide as
possible without wrinkling my brow, but that only makes
them water and roll back in my head. In the soft focus of
my fatigue, I catch dozens of Keith Richards winking at
me from the side of the road. There's not a car in front of
me, only a lone truck far behind. Damn, look out! I swerve

to avoid hitting a small furry thing. Harry's body swerves as well, sliding shoulder-first into the passenger door, his head following hard, thumping twice against the window. He awakens with a humphing sound.

"Goddammit it, Ruth!"

"It was an animal…an antelope or something."

"Where are we?"

I look at him like he's just asked our latitudinal co-ordinates. He lets out another humph.

"You drive," I tell him. "All this space is making me foggy. I'm liable to run into a herd of trees."

I pull over and sit still. As soon as Harry is out of the car, I lift myself over the console and settle into the passenger seat, slamming the door after him. He sits and stares ahead for a long moment.

"You know," he says, "Abbie once asked me—she must've been about fourteen—she asked me why a person would stay with you if they weren't married to you. She told me that we should get married, since I was around so much anyway—then at least she wouldn't have to feel sorry for either of us. Isn't that funny?"

"Is that supposed to make me feel bad, Harry? Because it doesn't." I want to say more, to argue, but I don't know what to argue about, and I don't know why I feel so sleepy. I don't know why I feel like crying. "Could you please just drive?"

Harry drives as he taps the trip computer screen on the dashboard, in between tapping the radio, in between tapping his phone, which sits on his right thigh. We listen to the Black Keys for all of twenty seconds, then Harry

touches the screen, switching channels. A Keith Jarrett
station, then Willie Nelson, Elvis Costello, Depeche Mode
(oh, God), and barely enough time to register each. He
switches his focus from screen to screen, two fingers gently
tapping one surface than another, continuing to tap as he
glances up at the road. It's imperceptible, the tapping and
looking a quarter inch right, then down, then ahead. He
has it down to a science, which makes the small ballet he
performs with those two manicured fingers even more
unbearable. Tap, look, music, music, tap, tap, tap, map, tap,
music. I try to will myself to relax and to accept a grown
man's obsession with directions and finding the perfect
roadtrip soundtrack. I mourn the death of folding road
maps and make a mental note to buy one at the next gas
station. Then we hit what can only be some kind of "no fly
zone," and the wall of psychotic sound turns to a hiss and
crackle. Tssssssstsssssss…c-c-c-shhhhhhhh…crrrrrrrrrrr.
Look, look, tap, tap, tap. I'm drawing blood from my lip. I
can't stand it. I smack Harry's hand with the side of my fist,
hit it the way a six-year-old might punch at a tormentor.
"Fucking stop it, Harry! For the love of God, stop. Stop
with the fingers and the tapping! Look at the fucking road!
You're going to kill me. Leave it all the fuck alone already!"

Harry doesn't look at me. He is so quiet now that it
seems he's stopped breathing.

I don't think that familiarity breeds contempt so much
as it does stupidity. I'm not contemptuous—just stupid.
Stupid for substituting Harry for nearly every fill-in-the-
blank since I can remember: personal reference, work contact, next of kin, person authorized to pick up your child,

person to call in case of emergency, person to contact in case you have to travel across the desert to find your dying mother and estranged daughter. I should think that *Harry* is the stupid one, for volunteering to be all those things to me, but I don't because I know better. It's not the money I've made for him, even though I have made him money and will certainly make him more. And it's obviously not sex—he can have that with the beautiful women with whom he occasionally becomes infatuated, only to dump when they start analyzing him in attempts at intimacy. He can score blowjobs from divorced women playing out their *Housewives of Beverly Hills* fantasies before the ink is even dry on their alimony papers. He can even enjoy the odd flirtation with a male rock star trying to revive his career with a tell-all autobiography. No, I know that Harry has been the one whose name appears on those annoying in-case-of-emergency forms because I have always needed and wanted him in a way that no one else ever has.

I have known Harry since that time in a man's life when he is the most fat with possibility and testosterone that he ever will be. I have remained constant in my regard for him: He is still, to me, the man he was back then—just as I'm still the girl I was to him back then. There, I've said it: I'm still a girl to him. I am still That Girl, frozen in time. Harry is the reason I don't have to look up old classmates on the web after thirty years in order to connect with someone who has me in mind as the teenager I once was. A woman I know once confided to me that, after her last divorce, she would sit in bed late at night with her laptop and a bottle of wine and look up old boyfriends. She knew that if they replied to her, it was because they still imagined her as her former full-breasted, dewy-skinned self, and not the woman with three teenage children who had sucked all the hair color and moisture out of her. Those old boyfriends would forever remember her not as the woman whose marriages were zero-for-two, whose breasts had been augmented once and lifted twice, but rather as the one who got away. So Harry is my Picture of Dorian Gray, and I am his. Dorian and Dorian, if you will—if that wasn't so true as to be utterly pathetic.

"Static is enough to drive someone insane," I say in an attempt to fix things—because an outright apology would mean that I'm wrong and sad. "Haven't there been studies on how static alone is a type of torture?" But Harry has yet to inhale. Quick, what else can I say? I stare at the road ahead, at the part of the concrete that looks as if it's melting into itself, the part that resembles a liquid ghost of a road. The skin on my forearms itches. A *Sesame Street* song pops into my head: about how skin keeps everything in, about how wonderful skin is no matter its size or color. Abbie loved that song, loved the images of happy kids playing in the sand on a beach circa 1980. Skin keeps our insides in. Skin is a wonderful thing. Should I ask Harry whether he can remember the exact words? I've got to think of *something*, and quickly.

"Harry?"

"I don't think you should speak now, Ruth."

Okay. I decide to check my comments instead. That's always a nice distraction for me: counting how many new messages of support and good cheer have arrived. It's comforting just to rub the phone between my hands. It's cool from sitting in my bag just underneath the vent. I flip it over and over, massaging it slowly—the same way I used to do with my worry stones when I was a kid—until it's the temperature of my hands. Until I can't tell the difference between body and device.

Sixty-two new comments. I scroll down the page without my reading glasses. The Es look like Fs, but I can still do well enough. Many of the comment names are recognizable: marymother, toddlerhell41, kookherroo, wearingspit02. I open some of the new ones, scroll down some more. Sam, Lorna…MissyC18. My glasses—I need my glasses now. MissyC. *Is* that a C? There must be lots of Missys, last name beginning with C. Missy C, born on the eighteenth of March, eighteen when I last saw her. For those first few years I wondered whether she remembered me, maybe all at once or little by little, like in a sci-fi movie when the hero starts seeing quick fragments of an alien past flashing in front of his eyes. But the more time passed, the more I hoped she wouldn't remember anything—me especially, the girl who pleaded with her to come to the last party she'd ever walk into.

With my glasses on my nose and my eyes closed now, I cover the screen with my hand. Abracadabra! I will now open my eyes with twenty-twenty vision and read something from someone named Missy, who will turn out to be an able, happy woman, previously unknown to me, with a couple of equally able and happy kids.

The message begins:

Believe me, I'm as surprised to be writing this as you must be to be reading it...

Missy Cataldo. Born on the eighteenth of March. Powder-blue princess phone.

sixteen

ABBIE

Eric's followed me home. Selma and Miguel will be here after they stop at the liquor store for a cheap bottle of Beaujolais. If, say, someone like the FBI had us under surveillance, we'd probably seem like boyfriend and girlfriend, waiting for the grandparents to meet up with us.

Eric stands slumped over his car door, running his fingers through his hair slowly and deliberately, as if he's trying to read his scalp. It's mesmerizing, somehow, watching his hands move, and the stillness of the rest of him. A strong breeze picks up, and just in time Eric tilts his head with his eyes shut to catch it on his face. Really strange. What is it about that gesture? I know: It's that I never see guys stop to greet the wind on their faces like that. Eric snaps his attention back to me, but now I'm doing my best Kristen Stewart scowl right into the sun. I can feel him staring at me, so I turn and glare back. "What?

What is it?"

"You…you're thinner than I expected," he says, almost apologetically. "And you seem much older than eighteen. But it's weird, your expression is the same as the one in your seventh-grade school picture, the one in *Girls' Guide to New Humans*." He lets out a small puff of air. "I like doing research, and besides, it's all on the web and your mother's blog. I'm always looking up stuff when I can't sleep at night."

"You mean, like odd facts about the weather?" I say, dryly.

He turns serious. "They definitely don't capture how fine your features are, or how dark your eyes are…the pictures, I mean."

"Really?" I say, trying to sound bored, but what I want him to do is keep talking.

"Yeah, you-you're—I mean, I could tell you were attractive, but you're even more…" he trails off. "They don't do you justice."

"Well, thanks, I guess. So, Eric, don't take this the wrong way—"

"I can't leave," he says as he collapses cross-legged on the gravel driveway. "Listen, somebody's gonna find you soon. You know, those chicks over at Jezebel are doing this major—"

"Oh God, are they at it again? You must've read their whole snarky 'Free Abbie' campaign from a few years back. Yeah, that would have been pretty funny, if you weren't me. You read that fake blog they set up? And that stupid cartoon of me as a dancing circus bear and my mother as the trainer? Really funny."

"They're tweeting from all over about Abbie Handler sightings. You know about that, right?"

I didn't, but instead of answering him I grimace and make an involuntary sound like I'm going to spit up a hairball or something. Eric grins.

"Why?" I ask him pointedly. "Why is that even interesting or remotely *okay*? And how big a loser do you have to be to really care?"

Eric shrugs noncommittally, but I'm committed to staying angry now. Just then, Selma's car speeds over the rise in the road, sending little spirals of dust up into the air—and I can't help but smile. Selma prides herself on not driving like an old lady—she drives fast with her seat slid far back from the steering wheel, the windows rolled down, her left elbow resting nonchalantly on the door. She's said that she'll drive off a cliff before she can't drive anymore. Her best childhood friend, Estelle, choked to death last week on a *prune*—and it wasn't because Estelle was talking and chewing at the same time, because Estelle hadn't been able to speak in years; it was because her head was tilted too far up, due to the way your spine curves as you age. She'd been staring up at the same piece of ceiling tile in the nursing home for months; then, one day, she just forgot to lower her head when she swallowed and choked to death. Good thing Estelle's friends at assisted living weren't tweeting. I can't help but think of it: *Jeepers, Estelle just #chokedonaprune and now #she'sdead.* Maybe I shouldn't complain.

Selma gets out first and then skips around to Miguel's side of the car.

"The good part of getting rid of a leg is that it gives the

girls an excuse to touch me again," he says.

Selma cups her hands around his face. "Oh, I don't need an excuse, boy-o."

It's soothing and painful at the same time to watch them. I can't help but wonder how they manage to keep their balance and their humor. Eric stares unabashedly at the two of them exchanging whispers and playful pokes as they stroll to the front door. Winnie steps out of the house with Claire.

"Sorry I'm late," I call out.

"Not a problem" Winnie answers. "I cancelled my class today. Just didn't feel like it. What the heck, right?"

"Who the hell are those women in your water aerobics anyway?" Claire goes off. "Bunch of goddamn sissies complaining about their hips all the time. Who doesn't have pain in their hips, for chrissake? And that instructor is the smuggest son of a bitch. Thinks he's God's gift to women over sixty just because he bicycles in that ridiculous spandex thing—tight like the sausage casing it is, with all the fancy Italian logos. He's a fucking *Polack* for chrissake. Doesn't he know that you can see every goddamn crease and bump in his pants?"

"Oh, I think he's very aware of that," Winnie says. "Anyway, everyone, come on in, but be kind of quiet, because Esther's asleep."

In the living room, Miguel introduces Eric to Winnie and Claire. "Eric is a friend of Abbie's," he says and then winks. "She couldn't keep him a secret any longer. Am I right, *mamacita*?"

Eric doesn't even try to look like he's not enjoying

himself immensely. "Eric," I say. "This is Winnie." *Now disappear.*

"This boy saved my life," Selma croons, putting a birdlike arm around Eric. "I almost died, I kid you not—just like Estelle with that goddamned prune." She gives them all the short version of Eric's heroics—a version once removed, irony substituting for fear. When she's done, they all straighten up and give him sober looks.

"Well!" says Winnie.

"Well, well," Anthony says, nodding.

"Well is right!" Selma sputters.

Winnie moves closer to Eric. "It's a good thing you were there, Eric," she says. "So how do you know Abbie again?"

"Uh, kinda through mutual acquaintances. But I feel like I've known her for years. You know how some people just feel immediately familiar?"

Winnie seems to be mulling over Eric's nonresponse when Grandma appears in the doorway, her blue cardigan over her shoulders, her hair pasted with perspiration to her head like a cloud of white cotton candy licked down on one side only. She leans on her walker, beaming.

"A party!" she says. "Park the cars…in…the bathroom. No smoking in the house. It's bad for your health. You should know that, Doctor Singer."

"Doctor…what? Grandma, this Miguel."

"Honey, you need to call him Doctor. I'm sorry, Doctor."

"But—"

Winnie shushes me. Apparently someone forgot to tell me the rules of this new game, the one in which Grandma decides who everyone is. So Miguel is now Doctor Singer,

Grandma's long-dead obstetrician, the one who delivered my mother.

"Abbie, you remember Doctor Singer."

"Sure, Grandma. Hello Doc."

Winnie slips her arm around Grandma's waist. Claire whispers in Selma's ear, who, in turn, whispers in Doctor Sing—I mean, Miguel's ear.

"Ah-ah-ah," Grandma says, "it's not polite to whisper. I used to have to remind my daughter. My daughter—her name is—son-of-a-gun her name. For God's sake, I know she was married to...*Justin*, and her daughter is *Abbie*, and she is..."

"Ruth," I say.

"Ruth, yes, of course. Ruth. Esther, that's me. Abbie, that's you." Then she smiles at Winnie. "Winnie."

"That's right, dear."

"Claire, Doctor...and you are?" she says, squinting at Eric.

"Eric. I'm Eric. I'm a friend of Abbie's—and a fan of your daughter Ruth."

"My daughter Ruth has a lot of fans," Grandma says. "Abbie never liked that very much, did you, sweetie?" Then she grunts, stifling what probably would have been more of a yelp. "Honey, may I have another, uh...purple people eater?"

I grab a plastic pill bottle off the table and shake one of the purple tablets into my hand. Winnie fills a cup of water and hands it to Grandma. We all wait for the pill to move safely down her throat as she bites her lower lip, trying to swallow back the medicine and the pain.

"Eric," she says slowly after a long moment. "Eric. What…is it…that you *do*?"

"I'm a filmmaker."

"So artistic of you," she says, nodding. "Tell me, what is it you do?"

"Documentary films are my specialty."

"I see. I see. Yes, yes."

"And hopefully I'll actually make a living doing it someday, you know?" he says, chuckling in a way that is totally self-deprecating. I mean, could he be blushing as well?

"Yes, of course!" Grandma says. She and the others watch Eric like he's about to tell them the key to the universe. He senses this and launches excitedly into his story.

"I've only done two so far. Short and on a real shoestring. The first was about twins—child prodigies. The second one I'm in the process of editing. It's about a woman, Sonia McQueen. You'll love this: She claims to be Steve McQueen's illegitimate daughter. I met her in a Directors on Directing seminar. She looks exactly like her father—who, of course was one of the greatest actors and all-around coolest people who ever lived."

"Oh! *The Thomas Crown Affair*!" squeals Selma, patting her heart.

"They don't make them like that any more, do they? Sonia claims that she was born to a Swedish model in Mexico about one month after Steve McQueen died. The details seem to correlate with the time and places that McQueen was known to have been in the last year of his life. It's an awesome story, really—short of DNA samples, there's no way to know whether she actually is his daughter or not, but it's become so much a part of Sonia's identity that she's about built her whole life around a man she never knew. Wild, huh?" Eric nods excitedly, his eyes wild looking in affirmation. "In a way," he continues, "it's like the opposite of Abbie—instead of having fame thrust upon her, Sonia's convinced that the fame that should rightfully be hers has passed her by."

I feel my face flush hot, but thankfully no one turns to me.

"Fascinating!" Selma gushes.

"Is she in movies, too?" asks Miguel.

"Sort of. She's slated to be one of the victims in a Japanese horror–slash–sci-fi movie shooting in Nagasaki this winter."

"I can't imagine that her father would approve," says Claire sternly.

"Nagasaki!" says my grandmother, and her eyes bubble up with tears, breaking Eric's spell over the room.

"Oh, honey," Winnie says, "let's get you dressed. The party will wait."

"Okay," says Grandma meekly, as Winnie leads her back into the bedroom. "But tell Doctor Singer not to smoke in the house."

"Of course, dear lady," Miguel calls after her. He puts his hand on my shoulder and whispers loudly in my ear, "You're doing fine. It's not an easy thing. Why don't you go outside and watch the sky." He consults his watch. "Eight minutes to sunset."

A few minutes later, Eric joins me on the patio and peers into the setting sun. I look over at him, but he doesn't look back.

"Wow, that's your grandmother in there," he says finally. "That's gotta be hard. Looks like you've got some good friends, though." He takes off his jacket and looks down at the white V-neck T-shirt hanging off his body. "I look like something that should be put out of its misery," he says ruefully.

"Listen, Eric—I don't have any money, so I can't pay you to go away. And I don't have a pistol, so I can't kill you. Oh, man, I really don't know what you want from me, but now is *not* a good time."

"You mean with your grandmother here and all?"

"Yeah, that's right. And it's really no one else's business." He nods. "Listen, I don't talk to my mother, I don't want *her* to talk about *me*, and I don't want to talk about her or me to anyone else. You understand? The truth is, I wish she wasn't even my mother right now."

"Wow," Eric says, frowning. "That's intense. I mean, I thought she seemed pretty cool, for someone her age. Man, that's…I'm sorry."

"Right. How would you know?" I say, almost relieved. "So, you'll leave?"

He seems to consider it a moment and then shakes his head no.

"Eric, it's not that I don't like you. Because you seem… you seem like a good person—and I'm a pretty good judge of character. And *they* like you, obviously," I add, gesturing toward the house. "So I don't think that you're going to be killing us and burying our bodies in the desert any time soon. But you could be *anyone*."

"I know what you mean," he says. "I don't come off as a threatening person."

"No, not at all," I say—and it's the truth, as long as you don't consider killer good looks threatening.

"Can I tell you a funny story?" he says, but he doesn't wait for an answer. "I…I had this foster mother who enrolled me in karate when I was ten, because I seemed *too* nonthreatening, you know—too gentle, is how she put it. I think she probably thought I was gay." He laughs, but more in regret than amusement. "She was taking care of me and four girls, and I think she was worried that I was lacking in kick-ass-ness. I really got into it—the karate, the discipline and routine and stuff—so in a couple years I was a brown belt. I was really good. But I didn't advertise it, because it was still a weird choice over team sports, you know?"

"Not so much anymore," I say. "My mother made me take karate for a while when I was younger. Huh. But you probably knew that already."

"Yup," he says.

"Well, I didn't mind. Actually, I liked the whole routine of it, too. But, I mean, what were the chances of my using a roundhouse kick on some psycho?"

"Right, that's just what I thought," Eric says. "But one day after school, my foster sister's boyfriend—this big Neanderthal of a guy, *twice* my size—tried to push her into his car. And she didn't want to go, so he punched her. I ran over and yelled at him, and he punched me in the face and called me 'pussy boy.' Yeah. He was screaming, my mouth was all bloody, so I swung around and kicked him. He fell over and hit his giant Neanderthal head on the curb. Man, it was scary. I thought I'd killed him, because he was unconscious for like five minutes, and for those five minutes I sat on the curb with his head in my lap. When he came out of it, he was okay, but he didn't remember anything—I mean grabbing my sister or hitting me. He started to speak, in this really soft voice—nothing like the way he sounded before. And he looked at me and told me that he was dreaming, and I was in his dream, and he didn't know why. But in his dream, I dove into a lake and rescued him from drowning. I realized that he was still in his dream, thinking that I'd just rescued him. It was really weird. I remember thinking, *Wow, if he just stays permanently in his dream, he'll be this nice, normal person, instead of some slime-bucket asshole.* Maybe that was the choice his mind wanted to make for him. Maybe he just didn't have the courage to be that nice or gentle in his so-called real life. And that got me thinking: Maybe we're never really who we think we are. You go around projecting a certain image that seems to make sense, and then something happens that scrambles that image or knocks it out of your head entirely. And if you're lucky, maybe you can make use of that moment. But—I hate to say it—I think most people are probably too scared of it, and can't wait to go back to being the same person they always were."

"The same as it ever was," I say.

"You like David Byrne?"

"'Life during Wartime' is my mother's favorite lullabye. So maybe what you're saying is that all my mother needs is a good bump on the head."

"Well, I'm a brown belt, so that could probably be arranged. But who do you want her to be?"

"I don't want her to be anyone. She is who she is. And I'm just…I'm not even interesting. I'm going to be a gerontologist. It's not very exciting. Nobody does TV shows about doctors who have eighty-year-old patients. I'm just… I'm…" And then it dawns on me who I am, at least to Eric. "The Leung sisters…Sonia McQueen…me. That's your thing, isn't it—girls with screwed-up childhoods? Great. And what's my freak quotient?"

"I don't think you're a freak."

"Of course I am. But so are you." I say, hoping he'll try to defend himself. I want to see him get angry, but he doesn't.

"Well, I thought that was clear from the start."

"Give me one good reason why I should let you stay."

Eric juts out his jaw, like he's truly deliberating. "I know the Heimlich. That's a good thing to know around the crew you run with."

Okay, that's funny, but I don't know what to do with Eric, and he's beginning to wear me down. Before I can answer, an animal calls out from the shadows like it's being attacked. We both hear it, but neither of us moves. A muffled scream from an entirely different animal stabs through the cries, interfering with the attack—the mother of the first animal maybe?

"Eric, what do you need from me right now?"

"You know what I need?" he says softly, in a way that gives me that weird *whoosh* feeling of stepping back onto a curb just in time to avoid getting hit by a speeding truck. "Right now, at this moment, what do I need? A shower. Would you mind if I took a shower?"

"What?!"

"Truth is, I drove fourteen hours straight to get here," he says. "Camped out in my car two nights. Not very comfortable."

He's *so* pushing it. He knows it, I know it. But he did save Selma from death by cheese croissant. "The shower's off my room," I sigh, because at this point, why not? "Careful—it's got two doors."

"Where does the other door lead?"

"Outside, to the garden. And the bathtub. The bathtub in my garden. Because there's no tub in the bathroom, okay?" I can't hide my exasperation.

"Okay—thanks," he says, just as the mauled animal picks up its cry, this time seeming much closer. Then: "I think that's your grandmother calling."

I rush inside and take a seat at the foot of my bed, careful not to crush Esther's feet under the comforter. "Grandma? Grandma?!"

She opens her eyes and blinks a couple times, the skin on her face smooth and hollowed from sleeping on her back. Winnie is standing over her, holding out pills and water.

"I'm so sorry, honey," Esther says with a small cry still

in her voice. "Did I scare you? I just needed…one of those little…pebbles."

She means the pain pills. She swallows the one I put between her dry lips with the water. She closes her eyes. "I'm glad you're here, Ruth."

"It's Abbie, Grandma. You're at my house."

"Ruthie, you're the only one who understood…such a horrible, horrible day. I know you loved Max more than anyone. Where'd he get that curly red hair from, sweet boy? Blood on your skirt…I'm so sorry. Always remember I love you, sweetheart."

My heartbeat quickens because I feel like I'm hearing something intimate and personal that wasn't meant for me. How is it that I could suddenly know less about my grandmother today than I did yesterday? I remember those fantasies I had when I was little—fantasies about the *other* family I knew my parents must have had, about the man my mother married in secret before my father, about the child Justin fathered while hitchhiking through Europe. I'd conjure up those fantasies while alone in my room, wishing them to be true, actually *seeing* my long-lost half-brother approaching in a crowded airport after a years-long search, imagining the scene so clearly that I'd find myself clasping my hands together, gasping in anticipation. But with the slightest hint now that one of those fantasies could actually be real, I hate having had any of them.

Winnie opens my hand and puts a glass of wine in it. "Something good about that boy."

What is she talking about? I concentrate hard on remembering the past hour of my life. "Winnie, we don't even know him."

"If it wasn't for him…" she says and starts to choke up. "Selma…I can't even *think* about it. Besides, we only know what we want to know about people anyway, right? Not that I need to be right. But I could be."

"Sure, Winnie, you say that now."

"Oh, don't worry so much, Abbie," she says, shaking her head. "It's all over so quickly." She smiles wanly and leaves the bedroom. I hear her return to the kitchen, where Claire and Anthony are listening to some talk show on the radio and drinking wine out of teacups. It doesn't count if you drink Chianti out of teacups.

A strong draft pushes the bathroom door slightly open, but there's no light on inside—the tiny room is pitch black. *Please don't let Eric be someone who showers in the dark—or worse, someone who stands naked in the dark after a shower.* Or maybe he's run off. That's it: Eric's let himself out the bathroom door to the garden, scaled the stone wall, and run off like a thief in the night. Good. He's probably gone with the silver Tiffany bracelet that I keep on the toothbrush holder, a gift from Grandma for my thirteenth birthday. I hope he did. Then I can prove everyone wrong about him, including myself.

"Hello?" I whisper, pushing the door open another couple of inches with my finger. The bathroom is empty, warm and moist like after a hot shower. It feels good on my face. A blast of cold, dry air pushes open the outside door, replacing the last volume of warmth, and that's when I see him. I can see Eric but he can't see me, because I'm hidden in the bathroom, crouching in the dark, and he's in the white porcelain tub, apparently having filled it with buckets of hot water from the shower, just like I do. Plumes of steam rise around him, pearlescent in the moonlight. He's smoking a joint while my cheap rosemary candles balance uncertainly on the cactus by his feet. If I turned on the light and he raised his head he'd clearly catch me spying on him, so I sit motionless on the tile floor beside the toilet, watching. Leaning back on my palms, I can feel the inlay of the tiny embedded diamond shapes under my fingertips. A strange afterthought, my bathroom: Miguel told me he added it to replace the outhouse that used to be on the property. The second owner's wife wanted the modern luxury, but her husband didn't want to give up his outdoor view while sitting on the can. Miguel was their contractor, and he added the bathroom and put in an extra door facing outside to accommodate them both. The wife was an agoraphobic craft fanatic who hardly left the house, so she had plenty of time for her dotty projects. She cemented broken glass, pottery pieces, and tiny ceramic tiles into everything—the floors, the walls, and, of all places, the top of the toilet seat.

Eric still hasn't moved. If I were someone else—someone cool and blasé, who had tattoos and pierced lips and wore wife-beater tanks in the middle of winter—I might be in the tub with him. I would walk over and take the joint from his hand, then lower myself slowly and stealthily into the water, and he'd move apart his feet to make room for me. I'd lean my head back opposite him and lie completely still, like I used to do when I was really young. Lying back in bed, I could make my breath so shallow, my body so

motionless, that I'd feel like I had no body at all. After a
minute or so, I'd be overcome with the sensation that I was
a rock rolling across a deserted stretch of beach, picking up
sand, building up speed until I *was* the sand and the wind
and the waves all pulsing at once in the back of my throat.

Eric balances the joint on the edge of the tub and slips
gently under the water. One…two…three seconds. That
would feel good right now, to be swallowed up whole by
all that liquid warmth. Seven…eight…nine seconds since
he vanished beneath. On twelve, he punches his head
and chest back up and lets out a long, ecstatic howl that is
answered by something wild in the distance.

"Abbie?" Selma calls. "Abbie?" I yank shut the door to the
garden. "Honey, are you all right?"

"Yeah, fine—I'm coming," I jump out of the bathroom,
quietly closing the door behind me like an overacting
mime, and realize I'm shivering.

"My goodness, honey, you're freezing," Selma says,
handing me a sweatshirt off the bed. "Take this. Are you
sure you're okay? I'm going to make you some tea. Now
what did I come in here to tell you? Oh, yes. There's someone at the door. He says he's your father?"

"Justin?"

"Yes, that's who it is! Oh, phew! You knew. I was hoping
it wasn't some uninvited crazy!"

"You sure his name is Justin?"

"Yes, honey. Isn't that nice? He seems lovely."

Esther opens her eyes in bed. With one long-rehearsed

wave of her good hand, she manages to push her hair into some semblance of a 'do, smooth the skin on her neck, and glide a pinky over her lips, erasing any sign of drool. "Justin here?" she asks, as though she's been expecting him. "How wonderful. We should have a dinner party. Ruthie, tell him to stay for dinner."

I give Selma an imploring look that says: "Should I tell her? Do I tell her again that I'm not Ruth?"

"That's Abbie, Esther. Let's get you dressed. A party sounds like a wonderful idea. Abbie, why don't you go say hello to your dad? We'll be right there."

seventeen

RUTH

The umbrella over our table is emblazoned with the Cinzano logo, but I can't imagine that anyone stopping here has ever actually drunk Cinzano. The three other round tables are occupied by obese families—possibly members of a traveling caravan en route to a noisy camping spot for an outdoorsy family reunion. Twenty feet away, the patio ends where the parking lot, with room for a half dozen cars, begins. Beyond that lies the dusty highway to God knows where. Harry exaggerates when he says that I cried out in the car like I was having a stroke. He's deposited a large cup of soda water, a bottle of Lipton iced tea, and a plate of steaming fried potatoes in front of me. I'm better now, though I have to admit that for a moment there I'd forgotten where I was, forgotten the day, forgotten that I was in a moving vehicle on a desert highway when I abruptly opened the door to vomit. It's cool out, but not cold enough to freeze vomit. Back on Long Island at this time of year, it would be cold enough. I remember Liam Voorhees puking on my mother's Ford LTD after dropping me off from a date during which he'd polished off a bottle of Mateus Rose and a pound of cheap brie. He'd taken me to one of those wine-and-cheese date places decorated in the faux-library style that was so popular back then, with shelves of old *Life* and *Look* magazines. Missy had suggested that Liam take me there. Missy of MissyC18 in my messages today, after having been lost for thirty years—lost, as though she slipped out of my pocket on the Long Island Railroad and fell like a nickel between the crack in the seats. Lost just like that. And now she's in my hand again.

Dear Ruth.

Believe me, I'm as surprised to be writing this as you must be to be reading it. It's me, Missy! I wanted to tell you that I'm really sorry to hear about your mother's illness. She was so glamorous. I liked her a lot. It's good that you're taking care of her. She's lucky. It's a hard thing to do and complicated, because mothers are very complicated.

I don't know exactly what my mother told people. My mother's been dead for five years. Funny, I'm still alive. I went into therapy after she died. I cried a lot, which I hadn't done since The Accident. I call it The

Accident just because I've always called it
that. Anyway, I cried and then I remembered
lots of things, everything almost. So I
called my Aunt Rose. You remember her, don't
you? She was anorexic and we thought how
cool that was to be old and anorexic. She's
still old. lol. And I asked her whatever
happened to you, since I could remember you
finally, and she said that my father moved
us away and didn't tell anyone where, and my
mom wouldn't let you talk to me. She said my
mom told you to go away when you tried to
visit because I didn't remember anything from
before the accident and besides it was better
that way!!! I'm so sorry about that. I didn't
know. I couldn't know. By the way, my father
is alive and well, and I still live with him
but he said he couldn't remember who you
were, which is a lie that I'll let him have.
I'm sure he was angry that you or Connie
weren't paralyzed instead of me. I got most
of the use back in my arms, which was good,
but sometimes I still jumble up words when
I talk and that's why sometimes people think
I'm retarded or something, which obviously
I'm not. I used to have dreams about being
under the water paralyzed, looking at the
bottom of the pool. I'd see Max there too,
but he was alive and had gills like a carp
and looked very happy. I always wondered why
you kept him a secret from everyone. I never
told anyone about him. But secretly I wanted
a secret like yours, then I would have been
tragic instead of just superficial :) .

I've been reading your blog. I actually com-
mented a few times but I used a fake name.
Hope you're not mad. It felt good to talk
to you even if you didn't know it was me. I
guess I wasn't ready for you to know it was
me. Also I read your first book. It's really
good but sad because it's about high school
and I'm sure that the pretty, jocky girl that
you call Janice is actually me, isn't it? My
aunt told me that the movie "Only Girl" was
made from your book. I rented it. It wasn't
as good as the book. Winona Ryder isn't very
convincing as Anais. But I like that Janice
doesn't die, even though she dies in your
book. I guess that means that I died, right?

It must be wonderful to have a daughter. I'd
like to meet her someday. You are a very
insightful writer. I'm really proud of you.

I live in Arizona. My parents moved here
because they heard about the healing powers
of the desert and sun, but I think that
only matters for TB patients. My life is
pretty good. I actually do a lot of fun stuff.
These days I'm taking ballroom dancing! The
instructors are these really great gay guys
who pick me up and twirl me around then plop
me back in my wheelchair. They even picked up
my wheelchair in a demonstration and it was
like the chair dance at my bat mitzvah, only
with hot buff gay men instead of sweaty boys
in polyester shirts.

You've been talking about me so much lately.
When you used to call me just M, it was like
I was a spy in some movie. I liked that. And
when you wrote my name and I read about your
mom, I finally felt like it was the right time
to answer you.

I remember when you liked science fiction. I
remember wanting to be as smart as you. I
hope to hear from you.

Love,
Missy

P.S. I found out Connie is married and lives
in Utah. She failed her bar exam five times.
Then she married a Mormon man and converted.
She has four children and he has two other
wives. Isn't life strange?

P.P.S. My spelling is so much better now!
Remember when there was no such thing as
spellcheck?

"Ruth, you have to speak now," Harry says, staring hard at
me, the Cinzano sign backward behind his head. "Come
on, Ruth. Jesus, I never thought I'd have to plead with you
to talk. That's funny."

But he isn't laughing. He's also trying hard not to show
how concerned he is. Unfortunately, he's too transparent,
and not practiced enough at concern to mask it. "Ruth.
Please."

"Missy…Max…my mother. It's nothing. Nothing you'd know about."

"Honey, I don't think there's anything in your life you haven't told me—or written." He attempts a laugh, but it stalls in his throat.

"It's no one's fucking business!" I blurt out. "I don't have to explain anything!"

"Easy, Ruth. Wait, are you being blackmailed?!"

"Jesus, Harry…"

"I mean, do we need to talk to a lawyer?"

"No, Harry. No. No and no."

"Ruthie, you didn't take another Xanax, did you? Did you?!"

I start to cry, but it's not the way my father would have wanted me to cry. My father would have wanted me to cry like Ingrid Bergman. My father used to say that nobody cried like her, that no woman could cry and still look as beautiful and classy as she looked when she wept. My mother would have rather died than cry around my father. I can hear the sounds coming out of my mouth, feel the way my mouth is moving, but it's like I'm trying to cough up a chicken bone sideways. Cary Grant would never have kissed Ingrid Bergman if she had cried like this—the way you cry when the only people who know the truth about you, about why you are the way you are, have either forgotten that truth or are long gone.

Harry looks…what is this look? I've never seen it before. Scared. Harry looks scared. Doesn't that just suck—that two people together with a rented car, under a Cinzano sign in the middle of the fucking desert, are scared at the same time? Goddammit. "Goddammit, Harry. Let's go! Let's get this over with. I want this to be over! I want to be sitting in my office, with the heat on, doing my life! Let's go!"

Harry stares at me for a moment longer than neccessary, then he grabs the keys off the table and heads for the parking lot. I follow him, hurling my cold fries and tea across two tables into the trash.

eighteen

ABBIE

Justin has arrived with love and moral support and no battle plan—as usual. He hugs me the way he used to when I was gawky and twelve—when he'd squeeze me too hard on my weekend visits, so he wouldn't cry at how quickly I was growing up. He can still lift me off my feet in his big bear hug.

"Da-ad," the word squeezed out of my chest because he's hugging the wind out of me. That's another reason he hugs me so tightly, to make me say "Dad." That's all that can come out when you're trying to make consonants without air: "Dad." I saw him a few weeks ago at his bungalow in a still-hippie enclave of Topanga Canyon. He'd like me to live there with him and his three decrepit mutts and revolving yoga practitioners, but I can't. He likes being surrounded by woods and lichen, but I need the desert now. He claims that I live here so I can see the enemy approach.

I know that deep down inside, he still cares for my mother, although he seldom talks to me about her because he knows I'll go all ADD if he does. He insists that she's always had the best of intentions. "That may be true," I've told him. "However honorable the intentions of someone can be when they dig up my diary after I've buried it in a Ziploc bag in the backyard." Which is where our discussions of Ruth usually end.

I introduce Justin to Winnie, Selma, Claire, and Miguel. I catch Eric out of the corner of my eye, appearing from behind my father and me, his hair toweled dry and combed back from his face. "Oh, and this is…Eric, here."

Eric pushes his hand through the others. "Sir," he says, taking my father's hand.

My father does a double take, probably because Eric isn't eighty or dying. Eric, for his part, winces like he's expecting some kind of unpleasant reaction. They stare at each other for a second too long.

"Eric, is it?" Justin says, like he's never said such a name.

"Yes, it is, sir. It's very nice to meet you!"

"You don't need to be so formal, Eric," says my father evenly. "Just call me Justin. That's what all my friends and *clients* do."

"Oh, Justin!" my grandmother calls weepily. "So good to see you. I've missed you. It's just…so good."

"It's good to see you, too, Esther." My father takes Grandma's hands into his and gently massages them with his big, double-jointed thumbs. "You're looking lovely. I hear that Abbie stole you out here for a little *retreat*," he says loudly and deliberately, apparently confusing her mild dementia and her cancer for deafness.

"Retreat," Grandma echoes. "I am. The last retreat. Shhhh. Don't tell anyone."

"I won't," he says, peering at me.

"Now all we're missing is *Ruthie.*"

The knock at the front door kind of stuns everyone into silence. Nobody moves—after all, the way things have been going, it only stands to reason that it'd be my mother. Claire tugs open the door, revealing Anthony in a new, pressed windbreaker and freshly washed and combed hair.

"Lookin' sharp," Winnie giggles.

Claire makes the introductions. Anthony shakes hands with Justin and Eric, then he bows slightly, clicks his heels together and waves hello to me. I wave back.

Justin turns directly to Eric, whom he's been eyeballing since he came into the room. "Eric?"

"Yes, sir?"

"Just wanted to make sure I got your name right. Eric."

"We've heard such lovely things about you, Justin," Winnie says. "It's really a pleasure to finally meet you."

"However, your wife—ah, I mean ex-wife—now *she* sounds like a piece of work," Claire offers.

"Claire! For goodness sakes," Anthony groans, "let's not scare the poor man off, shall we?"

"No, no, not at all," my father says. "I've heard much worse."

"I just call it like it is," Claire scoffs.

"Claire, let's not—"

"No, seriously," my father says, smiling his broadest, sexiest smile at Claire. "These days you have to assume everyone is crazy or medicated until proven otherwise. Am I right, or am I right?"

I brace myself as Claire considers this, because what she could have heard was, "I'm assuming you're crazy and medicated, right?"

"Ha!" she says. "I like that! The goddamned truth! Crazy or medicated."

Once again my father demonstrates that he can say just the right thing at the right time. Claire starts chattering away at him, regaling him with her own observations about the crazy and medicated. My grandmother whispers into Winnie's ear. Eric stands mute, watching Justin.

Anthony reaches into his bulging jacket pocket and walks closer to me. It's amazing how well groomed he is—his baby-blue and stone-white windbreakers always clean, cardigan underneath with all the buttons, a minute tear at the hem darned with matching thread. He's so unlike the old men who circle the senior center in town, the ones who walk with their heads down, watching their every small step, afraid of tripping and falling, and dying—the ones with food stains forming uneven, oily patterns alongside the zippers or buttons of their pastel-colored jackets. Anthony told me that he tried going to the senior center once, a few years back. He sat in on a bingo game, even though he had no desire to play. "I looked around," he told me, "and all I saw was a sea of gray. They were all so *old*. There was no sense in my staying." Which is funny, because most of the people making up that sea of gray were younger than he.

Anthony pulls a rock from his pocket and hands it to me. It's the size of my palm, dirty, pink-hued, and uncommonly smooth and round, with two appendages, one long and one wide. "Turn it with the crack facing up."

I do, and the rock is a teapot—a nearly perfectly shaped teapot.

"For your kitchen window, kiddo," he says. "It's a keeper, yes?"

"Yes. Thanks, Anthony. It's awesome."

"I'm gonna start you on your own collection. My legacy to you. You need to start something of your own—I mean, a ritual. God knows, if I add one more big one like that to my windowsill the whole damn house is gonna sink into the ground!"

Winnie sidles over to us. "Your timing is perfect," she says to Anthony.

"You're surprised?" he says, arching one eyebrow.

"Never," she says, apparently not referring to his timing.

"Eric," my father barks.

"Yes?"

"Excuse me for a moment, will you, Claire? I want to finish that bunion discussion as soon as I take care of something. I think that the *reiki* might actually be helpful, even in your case."

"I'll be here," Claire says.

My father goes to Eric and places a hand on his shoulder. Eric's whole body tightens as he leans into the touch.

"Whoa—relax, son. You carry a lot of tension in your shoulders, you know? That's my specialty, tension and re-alignment, peeling back the layers of the old psychic onion.

I could give you some exercises for that, but right now I could use a little help. You seem like a mechanical sort of guy. Am I right? I think I may have developed a slow leak in the old radiator on the way here. Christ, I can barely tell the distributor from the spark plugs. Maybe you could come out with me and take a look."

"Sure," Eric says, his voice oddly strained. "I...I'm pretty good at mechanical stuff. I can probably help."

"Always good to know someone who knows their way under the hood of an automobile," Anthony says. "I certainly couldn't help you there."

"Abbie, why don't you come with us? To the car. We can catch up while Eric does some fixing." To the others: "You'll excuse us for a couple minutes, won't you?"

They smile. They'll excuse him anything at this point, especially Claire.

ᗡ   ᗡ   ᗡ

I walk ahead of my father to his truck, an old pickup that he uses for hauling firewood and bricks. With the sun nearly set, we might need a flashlight. Eric trails along behind us, which seems strange because I'd imagined him wanting to turn on the charm with my father the way he's done with the others. Justin opens the hood and stares into the maze of greasy black rubber and metal.

"So, Eric," he says, without turning his head. "How's the old scapula? Giving you any more pain?"

It's happening again—people talking in encrypted language—the second time since last night. "Scapula?" I say, hoping Justin or Eric will laugh. *It's a joke, right?* "Scapula!" Neither responds or looks at me.

"No. No, it isn't, sir—Justin. Sir," Eric says. "You really fixed it."

"Good," my father says. "No pain like scapula pain. It was your scapula, wasn't it?"

"Yes—yeah, you have a really good memory."

"Wait, wait a minute," I say. "Stop. This is a game, right? I don't know this one. Could you explain it to me?" But the two of them seem locked in an eyeballing match, protected by an invisible force field preventing outside interference.

"Well, it hasn't been too long," my father continues. "Your last session was about a month ago, am I right?"

"Right. Yes."

"But Dr. Rosenbaum of Toluca Lake didn't really recommend you, did he?"

"No. No, he didn't, sir."

"And you really didn't have an old karate injury, now did you?"

"Well, actually, sir, I do. But it wasn't why I came to see—"

"You're a shrewd one, Eric, I'll give you that. So what did you do—rifle through my desk while you were waiting?"

"No, no, of course not. Totally not, I wouldn't think… that would be completely not cool…at all. No, I, uh…on your bulletin board, there was a card, in the envelope. A birthday card. Abbie's address was on it. By the way, happy belated birthday, sir."

I've forgotten to blink, so now my eyeballs are in danger of shriveling up in the cold air and falling out of my face. "Eric? What are you—what is he talking about? Justin, what's going on?"

Justin draws long, deep breaths through his nose like he does when he's readying himself for a particularly difficult asana.

"You guys, you're freaking me out!"

"Abbie, I just need a chance to say—and, Justin, sir, I really am everything else I said I was. You told me that I reminded you of yourself when you were much younger and more naïve. And I liked that. Yes, I did know that you were Abbie's father when I went to you and…and, Abbie, I didn't know how else to go about finding your address. She's…Abbie, you…you're like the most private person on the planet. Well, you know that already, and…you both do. And, by the way, I really did benefit from the acupressure and the herbs. And, um, I did take your advice."

To my father—someone who spends six weeks out of every year at a Zen monastery under a vow of silence, eating and drinking out of the same wooden bowl wiped clean after meals with a cloth napkin—nothing in the whole universe requires this much explanation. He tilts his head down so his pale blue irises are half swallowed under his lids, his gaze never leaving Eric, then he centers his weight in a stance that reminds me of wolves in National Geographic specials when they're deciding whether to sniff or devour a stray animal.

"You have to know that I mean Abbie no harm, that I mean no one any harm—that I am not a harmful person. If there's anyone who can sense this about me, it's you, Justin. I've never even gotten a traffic ticket. I mean—"

"Eric," my father says calmly. "I like you. I liked you instinctively when you came to me with your pretend aches. I liked that you recognized the Cindy Sherman photos on my wall. I watched that tape you gave me, your movie about the musical sisters. You're talented. And I agree with you about Nisargardatta's *I Am That*: 'Mind causes insecurity,' no doubt about it. So I want you to listen very carefully to what I'm going to say. If you do anything to hurt Abbie in any way, I will come after you and I will find you. And although Nisargardatta would probably disapprove, I will chop you into very small pieces and bury you in the Angeles Forest. Do we understand each other?"

"Yes, sir. Absolutely. Trust me, I would feel really bad about disturbing your vishranti like that."

"That's good, Eric. I think you and I really do understand each other."

"We do, sir."

"And I do, I really do admire this tenacity of yours."

"I appreciate that, sir. Though I do have to point out that Nisargadatta isn't entirely opposed to violence—doesn't he also he say that 'Existence implies violence… As long as you have a self to defend, you must be violent'?"

"Don't push it, Eric. Less is more." Then my father lifts his head and addresses me for the first time since coming outside: "Abbie, you do whatever you want with this information. I'm completely releasing on this now. My feeling is that you have nothing to worry about, but you've got to do whatever you feel the need to do. What are your feelings?"

"Well, Dad…"

"Yes, honey?"

"I need to go back inside now."

"Let's do it. Swami Eric, would you care to join us?"

"Yeah, yes, thanks."

My father leads the way. I'm almost afraid to look back at Eric—afraid that he'll look different now, that he'll have a tail and two heads or boils and blistering acne all over his chin and cheeks that I hadn't noticed before. How could I not have wondered how he found me?

"Abbie," he whispers.

I look at him and take in his beautiful, serene, unblemished face, shocked that he looks the same. I wanted him to have sprouted horns so I'd have an undeniable reason to lock him out.

"Wait a minute, Abbie—please," he says as my father continues into the house without stopping. "That was the only way I could find you. I did what I needed to do. Just like you—you did what you needed to do with your grandmother."

"That's different."

"No, no difference," he says, shaking his head. "I know what you're thinking. You're thinking that I'm the dipshit guy you should intuitively know to stay clear of, some soulless douchebag. You're thinking that I'm this opportunistic stalker asshole, but I'm not *that guy*. I'm anti-him. I'm the antiguy. I know who those guys are and I'm not one of them. I'm…I'm…"

"You're Antiguy."

"Right."

"Like a superhero."

"No. Of course not. I mean…"

"You're the *antidote* to those guys."

"Abbie, come on."

"You need to stop talking now. I know what you are. You're just another obsessive fan freak—the only difference is that you're not someone's forty-year-old mommy who loves my mother's blog, you're a *filmmaker*! Woo-hoo! A filmmaker! Bet you have the whole Criterion collection on DVD, don't you? You need…you know what you need to do? You need to crawl back in your emo-surf-boy spaceship and go home, wherever that might me. You're just pathetic. And a liar."

"I never told you any lies. I didn't tell you one lie."

"I've heard *that* before." It's weird, because I don't even half believe what I just said to him—I'm pissed, but I believe him. I stop at the front door and look back. "I'm only letting you stay because of Selma. It'd make her too sad to think that she was rescued by some…*asshole*."

The obvious hits me then, raising goosebumps up and down my arms—my own eight-month-long fiction, the one of me on a road trip because I can't bear to tell my mother the truth. Eric makes no reference to it, my lie. He could, instead he nods sadly and follows me back into the house.

Eric sits by Winnie, Selma, and Grandma. My grandmother greets him as if he was her-son-the-doctor. Claire chats with my father, who has certainly "released" on the driveway encounter. I've always been amazed at his ability to step out of anger—or any emotion for that matter—as easily as stepping out of a pair of pants. Occasionally one of the crew will look in my direction and nod in this weirdly serene way, like one cult member acknowledging another. Winnie, in particular, is so still and focused in her gaze that it makes me wonder whether she's trying to communicate telepathically. And why not? I concentrate on receiving her message. I try to clear my brain, but I can't stop the mad, free association of numbers and equations and Eric. I visualize the side of a red barn, like my father used to tell me to do when I couldn't stop obsessing. Red barn. Weathered, splintered red barn. Meditate on the lone red barn. Nope, no room for Winnie's message. Okay, now she's obviously frustrated by my inability to hear what she's thinking, because she's coming over with Anthony in tow.

"Let's go in the kitchen," she says.

"Okay." I move in slow motion after them, not wanting to disturb any vibrations that might still be trying to work their way telepathically toward me.

"Esther has been talking to us," Anthony says once we're standing as far away from everyone as possible without leaving the house.

"With great clarity, I might say," Winnie adds.

"Yes, yes, that's important. She has moments of great clarity. I can tell she was a sharp one, your grandmother."

"She still has her moments."

"Yessiree, still has moments."

"Right." This must be the part where they tell me about the key to my grandmother's safe deposit box containing the last known copy of the Declaration of Independence and the names of Oswald's CIA cohorts…or that upon my grandmother's death I will be whisked away to some here-tofore unknown Eastern European province where I will promptly be crowned queen mayor and sovereign ruler.

"Your grandmother would like a *party*," Anthony says.

"Yes, a party," Winnie echoes. "Her words."

"A party with music," Anthony continues. "She's told us her favorites: Michael Feinstein, Yo-Yo Ma, Tom Jones, and the Andrews Sisters…although I would have had her pegged as a Sinatra fan. I'd have put money on it."

"You guys, that sounds good. A party."

"A party with music, food, family, and a few good friends…and cocktails, dear," Winnie says. "I've done this before, Abbie. It's been wonderful. Something you never forget or regret."

"That sounds great. Why not?"

"Why not, indeed."

"I mean Grandma loves a good cocktail. She used to drink old-fashioneds and let me eat the cherries. Do you know how to make those? I think I remember. And grasshoppers—I read they're making a comeback at cock-tail parties—she likes grasshoppers, but only on special occasions. I think they taste like Girl Scout cookies." It strikes me that the vibe in the kitchen has become very somber, given the subject.

"Abbie, Anthony can get hold of the stuff for Esther's cocktail. We had a friend who went this way a few months before you moved here. Stanley. Stanley Price. It was beautiful and very peaceful. Very much a *celebration* of life."

"It's really just a matter of making the arrangements, dear," Anthony adds. "Your grandmother brought everything we'll need for her *cocktail*."

Her cocktail. Her *cocktail*—I mull over the word, repeat it under my breath, thinking it'll take on another meaning. Cocktail. A cocktail. Martini, Stoli, Cosmo, *Mad Men*. Molotov, Shirley Temple, Mickey Finn. Sedative, drugs, morphine…I gasp. "Oh, my God. Oh, I see. I understand. Oh, wait—"

"I know, honey," Winnie says gently. "Just sit with it for a minute."

"No, no, I don't really need to think about it. No. Thanks, though. She's not ready for that kind of party. But thanks. Really. Thanks."

Winnie blushes straight down into her turtleneck. "I know, I know," she says. "It's a difficult thing to contemplate at first—"

"But you should know that this is what Esther wants," Anthony says with an urgency that I've not heard before. "She's told us so in no uncertain terms, and she said the sooner the better. She's been thinking about this for a long time. A long time, Abbie. Better with us than alone with some plastic bag—"

"Alone with a *what*?!"

"Nothing. I mean, she knew you'd have *reservations*—"

"Reservations? No, no reservations. Just, no."

"She wants this," Anthony says. "You have to think about it, Abbie. Your grandmother wants this."

"She's here with us for a reason," Winnie adds. "There are no coincidences, no mistakes. It's all perfectly timed. Everything. It's why you brought her here. You just don't know it yet. But it's perfect."

"Perfect? What's perfect? *Dying?* When's that perfect?"

"Honey—"

"You-your husband's death…Lou's death was perfect?" I sputter.

"Yes, honey," Winnie says, getting a faraway look in her eyes. "Lou had a great run. We had a great time. I was lucky to be there. Esther had—"

"No, I'm sorry," I say, trying not to cry, "I–I can't…"

"It's not your choice, hon. It's not in your control. Your grandmother will find someone to help her. She will. But I think it should be someone she loves, don't you?"

"No, she can't go. She can't. There won't be anyone left to…to…for *me*…you know. She's always been there. She's not just my grandmother. I know, I know, it's not about me, but I'm not—seriously, she's not ready. She's *not*. She can't go. Not yet."

"Abbie, honey, I'm sure your mom—"

"No. No! My mother? I'm not…I can't even start…my *mother*?" I want to laugh like a hyena, even though the thought of my mother right now is definitely not funny. Oh, no, I can't help it, but I am…I'm giggling. We're talking about Grandma having a final cocktail and I can't stop giggling.

"Honey," says Winnie, putting her arm around my shoulder.

"This is so not funny," I manage to say between giggles. "I know it's not funny. I don't know what's happening to me. I'm sorry. What's wrong with me? I can't help it."

"I know, dear."

"I can't stop. Laughing. I'm sorry." I can only remember

a couple times when I couldn't control the muscles in my face. One of those times I wound up laughing at my uncle's funeral. I'd thought then, at the graveside, that what was happening seemed the opposite of having a stroke, because instead of the muscles in my face going flaccid, my cheeks were trying to pull away from each other in some kind of weirdly grotesque and uncontrollable smiling spasm, and it hurt to try to pull them back to neutral—like now.

"I know. It's all right, honey," Winnie tells me.

"Winnie, my mother—oh, God, not that my mother has a say, she doesn't—there's no way we can let Esther d-do *that*…or we can do that without…without her saying goodbye…a final goodbye to Ruth. You know? *Goodbye* isn't even like the right word, because it's not like 'goodbye, you know, see you later.'"

"Oh, well, if it's your mother you're worried about, you should know that Esther told me that she had a very vivid dream last night. You know, like Miguel's dreams, the way he visits his son in his dreams? Well, Esther felt quite certain that she'd alerted your mother. She told your mother to join us all here."

"She told my mother in a *dream*?" Thankfully, I've gained control of my face. "To come here?"

"Yes, dear."

"My mother doesn't even know where *here* is."

"She does now, sweetheart. Your grandmother told her. And it will all be okay. You'll see. She should be on her way."

I've always believed Miguel's stories about his dream visitations. They're so fantastic in a sort of Frida Kahlo–on–

peyote kind of way. But Miguel—mystic, sculptor, former world wanderer, and lefty radical—is not my Brooklyn-born Jewish grandmother, whose idea of transcendence is when a woman's face meets her perfect color palette. And my mother—I wouldn't know her whereabouts at this moment any more than to guess that she's nowhere east of the Pasadena Freeway. But I don't know that for sure. I mean, what if everyone is crazy except for me? What if everyone is *sane* except for me? Would I know either way?

"You know, the desert *is* a magical place," Winnie says. "Isn't that why we're all here?"

In the living room I hear my grandmother laugh, then cough. She coughs harder and leans forward to cover her face, because the coughing threatens to dislodge her dentures and send them flying across the room. She slides one hand under the top of her shirt like she's reaching to hold her chest together, convulses again, then yanks a handful of crumpled tissue out of her bra. A thin notebook smaller than a pack of playing cards slides out the bottom of her shirt and onto the floor. The coughing subsides.

"Okay. Okay," Grandma gasps. "Oh, oh, that...hurt." She spits blood into her tissue then squeezes it against her lips, looking frightened, trying to stop the leak. I run over with water and the pills she calls her blue pebbles. Claire picks up the notebook and holds it out to Grandma. "What is that?" Grandma asks.

"It's yours," I say, but Claire hands the warm, moist pad of paper to me instead.

"I don't...know that?" Grandma says. "Did you give that to me?"

"No. But I'll hold it for now, Grandma. Here, can you swallow this?"

"I'm okay," she says. "Stop. Stop fussing."

"Do you want to go to your room?" Winnie asks.

"No. Just stop. Finish!" It's an order. Grandma smiles at me with what looks to be her last ounce of her energy. But I receive it this time—her telepathic transmission. She means: *Leave me alone. Let me be. Bring it to an end. I'll die however I please.*

nineteen

RUTH

It's been thirty-five minutes since we passed a bleached-out, hand-painted billboard reading "Pray for Tucson." Harry has navigated this last stretch entirely in silence, concentrating only on the GPS screen and whatever he could see out the front windshield without turning his head more than ten degrees in my direction. He didn't want to make eye contact with me, but he wanted to keep an eye on me because he was worried. I could tell he was watching me beneath his classic prescription Oliver Peoples aviators. He's nearsighted, color-blind, and prefers driving at night. Abbie had a corn snake named Houdini, so, of course, she learned everything she could about snakes—they only see hues of color, they're very nearsighted, they see better at night, and they're very loyal to their owners. Snakes also have no eyelids.

"Welcome to nowhere," he says, looking straight ahead.

It'd be helpful now to rub some of my shamefully expensive eye cream on the red circles around my eyes, but, damn, I've brought the *wrong* shamefully expensive cream. I should have brought the serum for puffiness and not the antidote for dry-scaly. Serves me right. Nothing I can do except pat the minty yellow stuff over my entire face. Why didn't I bring the other cream? Goddammit. And why do I still think that the right cream makes a rat's ass of a difference?

"Hey. You. You better?" Harry barks, because if he speaks softly he might let on that he thinks something's wrong with me. "Because we're there in less than five minutes, that is if this car can make it over the fucking boulders of whatever nuclear blast caused this *neighborhood*, if you wanna call it that."

"Here," I offer Harry my .75-ounce pot of magic.

Without looking, he scoops out a mound of the stuff with his index finger and pats it over his cheeks and under his eyes. He smears the last gram of it between his middle finger and thumb and runs it through his hair.

"Ruth," he says gravely, "I will park the car. We will enter the house. You will say 'Hello, sorry we can't stay.' Then you will pack up Esther's things while I bring her to the car. You will invite Abbie for a visit, and we will plan a lovely brunch at Bruno's for the four of us in a couple weeks. My treat."

I'm so exhausted that I can't even manage an affectionate half-hearted "fuck you." I grab my prescription bottle and start to push down the childproof cap.

"Don't!" Harry yells, grabbing at the thing just as I

spring it open. We tug it back and forth, sending the pills flying around the car.

"Oh, Jesus Christ, Harry. Enough is enough!" I slam my feet on the floor as he pulls to the side of the road, then I peel two smashed tablets embedded in brown grime off the bottom of my shoe. Do I risk salmonella or plague?

"You crazy? Don't eat that," Harry says as he opens the door and tosses the bottle into a pile of gravel. "We're here. I'm taking control of this situation now, because you will just make a scene."

There's no curb, only a wide lane of gravel cutting a swath through desert expanse. Twenty yards or so from the road, a four-foot-high stone wall toppled in several places partially obscures a low-lying wood and stone structure. The wall, which wraps around the entire house, is clasped together by a wrought-iron gate, probably fashioned by some local recluse. In the dusk, the loops and twists of black metal seem in the shape of an Aztec warrior whimsically smashed flat by a sixteen-wheeler, with an equally smashed hawklike bird appearing to be feasting on the warrior's entrails. Tall, wrought-iron cactuses tower over the warrior and hungry bird. The structure, about the length of a trailer home, is apparently where my daughter lives.

"Okay, this might be trouble," Harry says, peering through the windshield at several cars parked aside the house. "It looks like she's got company."

"Who could she possibly have over?"

"How the hell should I know? Shit. Anyone with a cell phone could be trouble."

"So now what's the plan, Harry?"

"Hold on. Look." A young man emerges from the house. As he gets closer, I can see that he's the type of boy I would surreptitiously stare at from behind sunglasses at an outdoor café, or maybe smile at on a hike up Runyan Canyon if he was alone and smiled at me first and I'd remembered to put on lipstick. He doesn't see us, because we're hunkered down in the car and he seems preoccupied—he walks out into the yard a bit, then pulls out a joint from the pocket of his jacket and lights up.

Harry shoots out of the car with a grim air of purpose. "You stay put," he tells me. "I'll see what I can find out from the burn victim."

I'm a little uneasy with his tone. Harry's never been a fan of the marijuana community—he thinks pot smoking encourages lethargy and a general lack of focus. He approaches the young man like a cop about to roust him from a stoop.

"Hey, kid. Do you live here?"

"Excuse me?"

"I said, do you live here?"

"Um, no…why do you ask?"

"Can you tell me who does?"

"Who wants to know?"

"Listen, Stony, I've been having a really crappy day, and I don't feel like playing twenty questions."

"Neither do I."

"Good, then let's start again. I'm looking for Abbie Handler. Does she live here?"

The young man regards Harry carefully over the joint. "Who wants to know?"

"You really *are* trying to piss me off, aren't you? Now I asked you a civil question—"

"All due respect, I wouldn't exactly call it 'civil.'"

"Oh, you wouldn't, huh? You don't think this is civil? Because believe me, Stony—you don't want to see it when I get *un*-civil."

The young man frowns. "Is that a threat?"

"Just a word to the wise."

"Oh." His calm is like a lit match to Harry's gale wind. "Well, I've never really cared much for bullies, and I don't choose to answer their questions." With an air of regret, he stubs out the joint between his fingers and drops it in his shirt pocket, then puts his hands in his back pockets. "So if you'll excuse me—"

He starts to walk past Harry, who immediately seizes him by the arm. "You little smart-ass, who the *fuck* do you think you are?" But that's as far as he gets, because with the speed of a whip, the lovely boy turns and shoots a clenched fist in and out of Harry's face. A natural reflex, I'd say, considering Harry's demeanor—a breathtaking move, had I seen it in a movie. Harry only has time to cry out and bring his hands to his face before his body hits the ground like a plank. I scream and lurch out of the car. "Harry!"

"Arrggh…*God…damn…it!*" Harry moans as blood seeps through his hands, cupped over his nose. The young man kneels and wipes it away with one hand, while pinching the bridge of Harry's nose with the other. He instructs Harry to breathe through his mouth.

"I'm an EMT," he says. "Do as I say."

"Harry, are you okay?"

The young man looks up at me with a jolt. "Oh, shit—you're Ruth Sternberg. You're Abbie's mom! I'm sorry—is this guy with you?"

"He's my agent," I say, though the statement sounds ridiculous under the circumstances. It's not like me to feel queasy at the sight of blood, but I've suddenly got this sick feeling in my stomach along with a rush of adrenaline to my head. It feels like a jet stream of ice water pounding against my forehead, spreading into my scalp. In the distance, I see Justin and Abbie coming out of the house in extra-slow motion.

"Ruth?" says Justin, but his voice seems far away, and getting farther. And my thighs feel weak, like they can't hold up the rest of me. And my knees...

🖱   🖱   🖱

I open my eyes for a nanosecond—just long enough to see Abbie in front of me—then quickly shut them. Stupid move, I think, opening my eyes before my brain is in focus. If only I'd had the wherewithal to come into consciousness with my eyes closed, I could have listened to everyone like a fly on the wall before having to speak, before having to explain my surprise appearance.

"Ruth? You okay? Can you hear me? You fainted." It's Justin's voice, coming from my left, but I'm not ready to look at him.

"More ice!" Harry's voice on my right. Slowly, I pull myself to a sitting position on the couch.

"How did I get here?"

"Apparently Grandma summoned you in a dream,"

Abbie says dryly.

"I put you on the couch," Justin says, looking faintly annoyed. "After you fell."

"You carried me?" I ask

"No. I levitated you."

Before I can object, he shades my eyes from the overhead light and peers in them to check my pupils—making sure they're dilating, making sure that I'm not going to keel over—then, with his middle and pointing finger together, quickly taps twice on top of my head and the front of my shoulder. "You'll live," he says, backing away a little, just in case I decide to swipe at him—not that he has to worry, since my arms feel glued to my sides.

"Hello?!" Harry calls, pulling a baggie of ice off his face and handing it to an elderly woman with a gray pixie cut.

"Impatient son-of-a bitch," the woman says.

"Ruthie, honey. Welcome," my mother calls out from a chair packed with pillows. "We're having a little party."

"H-h-ho! Welcome! We've been welcomed! To the party!" Harry says. A gray and red bruise pulses under his left eye, underlined by a crusty streak of dried blood.

Another elderly woman—this one prettier than the first, her white hair in a neat topknot—offers Harry a tea-cup. "Here you go, young man," she says. "This'll help the healing process. Rosehips and valerian root with a touch of catnip."

"It smells like shit," Harry growls. "I need a mirror."

The woman with the topknot whispers into Abbie's ear. My daughter nods and shifts her gaze from me to Harry.

"Mir-ror. I said I need a mirror. A *looking glass*?" Harry

says. "Anything like that here?" No one answers Harry. *"Wagon train come in with supplies this month?"*

Pixie cut returns and drops a new bag of ice in Harry's lap, then turns to me. "Abbie tells us that you write a very popular blog," she says. "Although I don't understand the allure of writing your diary for the whole world to see."

"Abbie…what? Are you a nurse?" I ask. *Who the fuck are you?* is what I really want to say.

"Ha!" she says. "Abbie says you make a lot of money from it. So, I'm really curious—how does that work? And how would anyone know if you were just making up a bunch of crap or not? That's gotta be liberating, though. And they pay you for that?"

"I–it–it's not a diary. I'm a writer."

"Yeah, yeah, pop culture," she says. "Mass-market sort of stuff. I know the lingo. I'm more a Eudora Welty gal myself. Must be a generational thing."

I'm totally at sea. "Abbie, who are these people?"

"Mom, this is Claire. This is Winnie and Anthony. They're my friends. Oh, and that's Eric," she adds, pointing to the young man responsible for Harry's present condition.

"It's a pleasure to meet you, Ruth," Eric says immediately, holding out his hand. "Although it's like I know you completely already." He turns to Harry. "I'm sorry that things got physical, but you won't have any permanent mark, I guarantee it—as long as you do the Advil for twenty-four hours and keep the cold pack on a little longer. I really am an EMT. That's my day job." He takes out his wallet and shows us a California-issued paramedics license.

"Well, that's very fucking reassuring," Harry says. "I'll

bet you make shit at that job, right? Lucky for you—it means it's probably not worth my time to sue you."

"Oh, don't be so ungrateful, Harry," Justin says. "That shiner should make you a big hit at your next cocktail party—especially in the Armani." He holds a hand out for Harry to shake. "Long time no see."

Harry sucks in his cheeks and looks at Justin sourly. "Yeah, for sure, *Big J*," he says. "Say, how's the achy-breaky psych business going?"

Justin leaves his hand out a moment longer and then promptly withdraws it. "You really ought to write, Harry," he says, returning to his chair. "You've got such a way with words."

"Ha, funny, I've always thought that about you. Oh, wait. You *used* to be a writer. Right. I forgot. It's been so long."

"No, no, no, no," I say. "We're not doing this. This isn't any fun."

"Who says it's not fun?" Harry says, and Justin sniffs out a half a laugh. "See, Ruth, you seem to be the only person here who's not having fun." He looks around the room at all the old people staring at us. "I'm sweating like a pig here. What is this place, some sort of bunker? I'm going outside."

"Can I give you a hand?" the old man named Anthony says, offering Harry his hand.

"Thanks, Pops—you're a big help. And Ruth? While I'm gone, why don't you do what we came here to do? Remember?"

What we came here to do. At this point, I'm not sure

what that means. "I will, Harry."

The old man leads Harry out through the glass door to a patio hung with tiny tiki lights and eases him into a plastic lounge chair.

A moment passes. "So how…how did you find us? Justin wouldn't have told you—" Abbie says, but I cut her off.

"No, no, Justin wouldn't and didn't—but he should have, because it cost Harry a small fortune to find out. Thanks, Justin. Thank you very much. And thank you, Abbie."

"What do you want me to say, Ruth?"

I can think of lots of things, but I'm too tired to respond. Meanwhile, my mother is looking at me with the kind of look she reserves for small, dead sparrows. I hear Harry's cell phone ringing in the distance—some obscure, dissonant jazz piece that he doesn't even like but chose for his ring tone in order to illustrate the weight and depth of his character. The old guy returns, closing the patio doors, leaving Harry alone to yell at his phone. "Well. This is quite the reunion," he says, returning to the room. "Abbie tells us she hasn't seen you since last June! Can that be?"

Justin starts to laugh. "What?" I ask him. "*What* is funny? Oh, no, let me guess. It's all funny, because we all don't really exist. It's a dream. It's all one big cosmic jo—oh!"

I don't finish because I have to stifle the embarrassing cry in the back of my throat. It takes me by surprise, and I must seem a little scared by it, because Abbie regards me with an unexpected look of empathy on her beautiful, unlined face—a look inherited from her father. And what did she inherit from me? Only her stubbornness and her eyes—heavy lidded and set far and slightly unevenly apart. She's narrow where I'm wide and wide where I'm narrow. Her hair is black, while mine is twenty-seven expensive and painstakingly applied shades of blonde. The wave of our hair is the same, though—strands hanging in straight lengths, breaking into corkscrew flourishes. If we were in the same class in high school, I would want to be Abbie's friend. I would do whatever was in my power to make her my friend. "Abbie?" I hear myself saying.

"Are you okay, Ruth?" she asks.

"You got my dream, didn't you, honey?" my mother says.

I must look confused, because the woman with the white bun answers for me: "She certainly did, Esther. She must have."

"Obviously," the old man says.

That does it. I have to get out of this place. "Abbie, bring your grandmother's things. Mother, we're leaving. I'm glad that you and Abbie have been able to spend some time together, but now you and I are leaving."

"But Ruth—"

"Please, Mom, no arguing, because I'm not in the mood." But nobody moves; instead, they all sit there staring at me. I feel the situation already slipping hopelessly out of control. "Is everyone deaf?! Hello! Leaving! I'm speaking English!"

The other old lady turns to Abbie and clucks. "You're right," she says. "She's *very dramatic*."

Okay, fine—I'll do this myself. I look around and see

a closed door. Since it's the only closed door in the place, I figure it must lead to the bedroom. And since it's clear that no one else is going to do it, I run in to grab Esther's things.

The door slams behind me a moment later, but I don't have to turn around to know who it is.

"Ruth, wait a minute. I have something I want to say—"

"Oh, for God's sake, Abbie, don't start in."

"No, I—"

"And *please* don't tell me how terrible your childhood was. You got everything—"

"I know, I know—I got everything a kid could want."

"*Everything.* More than any other child—"

"And how would you know that?"

"How would I know? How would I know?! I was there!"

"No, you weren't. You were so busy trying to figure out your Next Big Move, you missed my life. You missed it and now you're old!"

"OLD!? What?! I'm not old!" I cry, feeling the hair stand up at the back of my neck, as though Abbie's words might instantly propel me into advanced old age—those words from the little girl who would hold my face in her hands, assuring me that I'd never grow old. "What are you talking about, old? Look at your friends! You wanna talk *old*?! You were *born* old."

"You don't even know what you're arguing about," Abbie says with a disgust in her voice I don't ever remember hearing.

"I'm not old! You're being mean!"

"You're like…you're like a *sieve* trying to hold water—you can't hold a drop. You can't stop yourself from saying everything on your stupid mind, everything you think, everything you want."

"Abbie, that's completely untrue—"

"I so hate to say this…but…ugh, forget it."

"What? Forget what? Finish!"

"Nobody even *likes* you. They may like what you write, but they don't like *you*. That's the truth. My teachers especially. They all thought—"

"What are you talking about? Your teachers loved me!"

"No, they didn't. They were just scared that you'd tweet horrible things about them or blog—"

"God, Abbie, now you're just being retarded."

"Oh, my God, I can't believe you just said that. *Retarded*?! What are you, twelve?"

"That's right, Abbie. I'm twelve, and you're the grown-up here."

"You're such an idiot, Ruth. I've known it for a long time."

"*What?!*" Abbie has never called me a name, ever, and it makes my scalp sweat. "What are you talking about?"

"Everything! Did you know that from the time I was four, I knew where you kept my Christmas gifts hidden?! Did you know that? Did you?"

"*So what?* What are you *talking about*? What do *Christmas gifts* have to do with anything?"

"Can't you guess?"

"I wrote an article about it once—"

"That's right, Ruth! *You wrote an article about it once—*

duh! You thought I wouldn't overhear some parent talking about how cute it was, your article about stashing my gifts on the top shelf of your bathroom closet—which you thought I wouldn't dare look into because I couldn't reach the light? The light?!"

"I loved that piece! And don't you dare call me an idiot. So you spoiled your own Christmas—"

"*You* spoiled my Christmas, Ruth. I couldn't open *Christmas presents* without you writing an article about it. I even got emails from strangers congratulating me on having my period! All because you never came up with another decent idea for a novel! You were done—you didn't have it in you, so you made me into your lab rat instead! It was painful. All of it. Did you ever consider that?"

"Painful? You never said—"

"Couldn't you tell?! Oh, my God! I didn't even know *how* to say it in the beginning, because I was *that young* when it started to hurt. And then overnight it got beyond words, and I kept thinking that if you loved me enough, you'd see how painful it was. I shouldn't have to tell you. If you weren't smart enough to see it, then I couldn't tell you. You thought my stomachaches were from worrying about grades? *Grades?* I could have gotten those grades on automatic pilot! I would have gotten those grades with my brain in a sling! You were supposed to know—by intuition or osmosis or *something*—because you're my mother! How could you *not know* that it hurt?"

"I never, ever…" I felt genuinely bewildered. "I never thought of that. Never."

I never thought of that. That must sound crazy, I

know—not realizing something so painfully obvious. But it's as easy as walking in and out of your house, week after week and year after year, and never noticing what color the foyer is—not seeing it until someone asks. That happens… it *does*, and it happens to people who aren't bad. It happens to people who love and are loved.

It suddenly dawns on me that Abbie is only a year older than Missy was the last time I saw her. I would never have talked to Missy the way I'm talking to my daughter now. So how do I talk to my daughter? How would I have talked to Missy if I wanted her to feel better? If I had a minute by myself to think, I could remember and then I could fix this. What would I have said to Missy at eighteen? *Quick, think.*

"I swear, Missy—" I blurt out.

"What? *Missy?*" Abbie screeches. "What is *that*? Missy? Is that code?! Do—do you even know my name?"

"Of course I know your name!"

"Well, congratulations, *Mom*!"

"Jesus, Abbie—"

"You know what kills me? When it comes to mothers, *you* lucked out! You had it *so easy*—"

"Easy?" I could tackle her and take her to the floor for that. "*Easy?* What do you know about my life?"

"I was there, remember?"

"Not for all of it! Not even for the *half* of it!"

"You had no reason…" Abbie sputters. "Grandma would never, *ever* have agreed—God, I can't even *believe* it—to have you *tweeting* about her…*in the end*. And *pictures*—are you that desperate? She'd be the last person on earth to want that! You were just bringing her home to—to—*take advantage* of her. Can't you see that? *What is wrong with you, Ruth?!*"

It's frightening, because I can count on one hand the times that Abbie has ever yelled at me. Even as a child, she never yelled. *Where did that sound come from?* I feel a chill from an open window…or maybe from a hole in the ceiling. I shudder uncontrollably and scan the room, compelled to find the source of that draft like my life depends on it.

"You're not even listening to me!" Abbie says. "How do you do that?!"

"Not listening?" I say, snapping to attention. "I've *been* listening. My whole life I've been listening! That's all that I know how to do! Don't you understand that? I listen to everything, anything. *Everyone.* And you know what? I'm sure Esther couldn't give a shit if I blog about her. How's that for something to listen to? I'll bet she couldn't care less. Because she trusts me! And because…because I *earned* it!"

"You're so evil," my daughter says.

"Go ask your grandmother."

"You're a *freak!*"

"Go ask her! Your grandmother would say—you know what she'd say? She'd say, '*Blog-blog-blog, silly girlie, what-ever that means. You do whatever you need to do, honey.*' I guarantee you!"

"Of course she would, because she's in no state to realize that you'd just be *using* her—just like you did with me!"

"Abbie, that's what humans *do*! That's what we're *sup-posed* to do unless we choose to live on a desert island! Some-times it's the same thing as love or help or manipulation.

Sometimes it's all the same."

"You really believe that, don't you?" says Abbie, turning away in disgust.

I need to stare at her face—however angry it is—for as long as I can before she goes away for another huge chunk of time. There are new angles to her jaw, and the corner of her mouth is twitching like it used to when she was eleven and just learning to hide her disappointment in a friend's apparent thoughtlessness. Her hair is parted differently— to the left of the part I used to impose when she was eight. I *am* old, I realize. My God, I'm old. I can't even look at my daughter without the virtual photo album of her childhood clouding my sight.

"You're sad, Ruth," Abbie says pityingly, "with your stories. I don't care if they're true. You just never knew how to be happy."

"Happy. *Happy?*" I say, my face twisting into an odd, old smile—because *happy* has always been one of those words that, if you say it enough times, makes you giddy, just by the sheer absurdity of it. "What is that? And what's to write about if you're *happy*? 'Happy' inspires nothing, sweetheart. Nothing. So I guess you're right."

"Now I know you're crazy," Abbie says.

"No! Absolutely not. Believe me, you have no idea what crazy is. No idea. I don't do crazy. That's the one thing I'm not."

"What makes you so sure of that, Ruth?"

Because of a sudden ruckus outside, I don't have time to answer. It's Harry, screaming: *"Ruth!! Goddamn motherfucker—Ruth!!"*

I rush through the bedroom door and catch Harry ricocheting across the living room, holding the back of his neck with one hand, his phone still in the other, his punched eye swollen nearly shut.

"*Arghhh*! Something *bit me*!" he yells as he zigzags across the room, his hands pasted to his neck and phone. "It *fucking bit* me! OH. MY. GOD!"

Justin tries to catch him by the shoulders, but misses. "Harry," he says. "Harry, stop. Let me see—"

"Black fucking widow! It *had* to be. Fuck, fuck, *fuck!*"

"Oh my God, Harry—" I offer, then quickly clench my mouth shut for fear of laughing out loud.

"Stop. *Stop*, Harry," Justin says, reaching Harry just as he's about to bounce off the bedroom door. "Stand *still!*" He puts his big hands on Harry's shoulders and leans his weight on him to hold Harry in place.

"What does it look like?!" Harry hisses. "Goddammit, I can feel it swelling up. It's stinging. Goddammit, it's stinging. Oh, God! The poison is racing through my veins already!"

I want to laugh. So does Abbie. We both cover our mouths in the same way, left palm over right hand. *Speak no evil...*

"Not fucking funny, Ruth!"

"It's not a widow bite, Harry," says Justin patiently. "As long as your throat's not closing up, which it obviously isn't, you'll be all right. Take a deep breath."

"Arghhhh, it stings like a motherfucker!"

"Enough with the swearing," my mother says.

"That's it, Ruth—I've had it," says Harry, breaking away

from Justin's grip. "I need out of this madhouse. I'm driving to the airport right now. I'm sure there'll be a flight, and I'm on it. You need to come—with or without your mother, I don't care. But we're leaving."

"Not yet, Harry. Not yet!"

"I'm not staying another minute! Ruth, do you hear me? It's toxic here."

"That's very funny, coming from you, Harry," Justin says.

"Blow me, Justin."

"Harry, can't you just—"

"I'm not doing this."

"*Please?* Can't you just wait—"

"Sure, I'll wait. I'll wait the two minutes it takes to walk to the car, put on my seatbelt, and stick the key in the ignition. Two minutes, Ruth—so say your goodbyes. I'm serious, Ruth. I might be dying here. Seriously. I'm serious as cancer. Are you coming?"

I don't answer him—no one does—so he turns abruptly and stalks out the front door. In the silence that fills the room after the departure of Hurricane Harry, Justin looks at me and says, "Don't you think you better go with him?"

"He won't leave me," I say. I know he won't. He'll sit in the car and breathe out the embarrassment of having lost his cool in the company of strangers, but he won't leave. He'll check his messages to find that little Miss Peace Corps has called to discuss her author picture, but he won't leave. He'll find out that there's a brushfire in the canyon next to his, but he won't leave. He'll just find something else to fixate on until I join him.

"He's leaving," Eric calls out.

No, he's not. I leap to the window in time to watch the Leaf taillights fade into the night. "Harry!" I yell from the front door.

"Harry!" I yell into the night as I start running after the car. *"Har-eeeeeeeee!"*

I can't see my feet hit ground in the dark, so I pound the gravel extra hard to make certain they do. The crunching of pebbles underfoot becomes like a chant, keeping me company, urging me on—crunch, go, crunch, step, crunch, go. Any minute now I'm sure to stumble on him, parked off by the side of the road, stewing in his seat. It's pitch black to my left. To my right, the blackness spreads like an ink spill over what little is left of a sky that was once a magnificent robin's-egg blue.

Finally, I slow to a stop. My mantra has ended. So, it appears, has civilization. Harry is gone.

twenty

ABBIE

I feel very tired all of a sudden," Esther says, as I sit her down on the bed, then pull her legs up and tuck them under the blankets. It's only been a couple minutes since Ruth blew out the front door yelling Harry's name.

"It's totally fine, Grandma. It's been a long day. A lot of excitement, that's for sure. You should rest now."

"Don't worry about me. It's your mother—" Grandma says. "She seems very upset. Is she all right?"

No, she's hysterical and totally psycho, is what I want to say. "Yeah, she's fine, Grandma. She just needed a little air."

"Where did she run off to?"

"She ran after Harry."

My grandmother shakes her head, then leans back on the pillow and shuts her eyes. "Girls shouldn't run after boys," she says, which makes me laugh.

"I'll remember that."

"Ruth," Grandma says. "Forgive her."

"It's me, Grandma—Abbie," I said. "Ruth's gone."

"I know," she said. "Ruth. Forgive *Ruth*. You're not listening."

It's as though whenever Grandma closes her eyes, someone rifles through and rearranges her life story—or doesn't. She returns on the page she left off—or not. She'll close her eyes on page one hundred thirty-seven and wake on page fifty, or one-thirty-eight, or maybe three pages earlier. She's reading from her own script, just not in order.

I've always loved my grandmother. She was exactly who you'd want a grandma to be. If that means perfect, then I guess she was perfect. My mother would sometimes say that Esther "remade" herself. I asked her what she meant by that the first time she said it, when I was about seven—it sounded like making the bed. "'Remade,'" my mother answered, "means that Grandma was someone else once—someone different to me than she is to you. And she was someone else to the people she knew even before us. But things happen to change people, and then sometimes they have to remake themselves. What matters now is just that she's *Grandma*—who loves her granddaughter more than anything else on the planet. Do you understand, honey?"

I said I did, but I didn't really, and I didn't ask again. I figured that was one of those things that adults can't explain any better—like why they say things like "Good job" and "Nice work" to people who really haven't done a good job or nice work. If it weren't my mother I was talking about, I'd say that she was being less than forthcoming, protecting my grandmother somehow. But that doesn't follow my mother's genetic code. I wonder—does my mother also know about Grandma's teen exploits to the accompaniment of the Andrews Sisters' "Hold Tight"? That was one of those songs that Grandma used to sing to me when I'd ask what her favorite tunes were from the "old days." *Hold tight, hold tight, hold tight hold tight brrrreackasacky want some seafood, mama? Shrimp and rice, they're very nice...* "Want some seafood, mama?" Was that a euphemism for something else? In the end, I never asked my grandmother how she "remade" herself, because her motto has always been: "Never explain—your friends don't need it and your enemies won't believe you." But what about family? What about explaining some things to me?

The silence that greets me in the living room is a little awkward, but it's an old, familiar silence. It reminds me of the reaction that my mother's friends would have at one of her cocktail parties after asking me how I felt about being in her latest book, or such-and-such magazine. I'd answer with some variation of, "It makes me feel nothing," and then there'd be this same silence.

"Grandma's resting," I say to everyone.

"Good. Good," Winnie says. "Anthony was going to go after your mother, but Justin said we should give her a little time to cool off."

"Where's she gonna go?" Claire offers. "Mr. Big didn't look like he was waiting for anyone."

I look at my father. "Not that I'm worried," I say, "but

maybe you should go after—"

"Another few minutes," Justin says to me, meaning that we should let my mother run out of steam before attempting a rescue.

"We'll play it by ear, then," Winnie says. "Interesting— we were just talking about how big emotions can sometimes make you lose your appetite, and other times make you ravenous. Would anyone like a BLT? I brought all the ingredients, including avocado."

"That would be a BALT, wouldn't it?" Anthony observes.

"Or ABLT," Claire says. "You're certain it wasn't a black widow?"

"Ninety-eight percent certain," Justin assures her.

"Mmmm. Okay, good," the others murmur, just to feel some vibrations in the room.

My father is daydreaming out the window now. "Justin? Justin?" I say, but he doesn't seem to hear me. "Daddy?"

He turns to me, looking puzzled, probably because he hasn't heard me say "Daddy" in a dozen years.

"Honey, she is who she is," he says, even though I didn't ask. Which is exactly why I never discuss my mother with him—because he reacts in that same preemptively knowing, forgiving way that ends the conversation before it can begin. "I'll go out and see what I can do. Be back soon."

He closes the front door silently behind him. Always silently—I've never known my father to slam a door. He's always made a stealth exit, without creating so much as a ripple in the air. Ruth, on the other hand, takes all the air with her when she makes an exit. When she's with you, it always feels like there's extra oxygen in the room; then she leaves and you're gasping for air.

"Just going outside for a bit. Be right back," I say to the room and notice there's someone missing. "Um, where did Eric go?"

"Oh, his phone rang. I think he went out front? Selma, did he go out front?"

"I think so."

"Okay, I'll be out back." I've got to get this straight, who to worry about first. Ruth? Grandma? And then there's always fanboy out front, who keeps interrupting my thoughts like so many infomercial breaks. It doesn't help that every time I come out of one of those breaks, I seem to experience a moment of temporary amnesia.

I stand on the edge of the dark patio with my eyes squeezed shut. *Abbie, concentrate. Just concentrate...*

"On what?" Eric says.

"What!?" I look over to find him sitting cross-legged next to a tiki light. "Have you been sitting there this whole time? I didn't ask you anything."

"You just said, 'Just concentrate,' and I said, 'On what?'" He gets to his feet, putting his hands in the air like he's surrendering. "You must have been thinking out loud."

"You're like Where's Waldo?—you're everywhere." I stare at him with my poker face. *Everywhere I don't want you to be.*

"Abbie, listen, I'm sorry. I'm sorry for the way I found you. I'm not sorry for finding you, though."

"Eric, what are you doing out here?"

"Just...reading," he says, somewhat embarrassed, holding up an ancient *Reader's Digest* that he's apparently fished out of the musty wicker magazine stand in the living room. "I haven't seen one of these in a while. I loved *Reader's Digest* when I was a kid. I actually thought the stories were kind of *exciting*, you know?"

"Exciting."

"Yeah. You know, for an eight-year-old. You ever read the one about the girl in the Mustang? She was driving her car when she was struck by a bullet fired from three miles away. By the time the bullet reached her, it was traveling at a speed just a little faster than the Mustang, and entered her brain just behind her left ear. The bullet missed all the other traffic and drivers and had just enough momentum to come in through the back window of her Mustang and kill her. One of those total flukes in life. I still think about that girl. I remember wanting to write to her family to tell them how sorry I was, and that I hoped it wouldn't make them bitter and angry for the rest of their lives. Isn't that crazy? But it's just the way life is sometimes—you can't live that same scene over and over, 'cause then you cheat yourself out of what's going on now."

"Yeah, well, it's probably a lot easier to think that when you're not personally involved," I tell him. "Didn't you ever see *Groundhog Day*? What about doing the scene over and over until you get it right?"

"That's just a movie, Abbie. No one's Bill Murray in real life."

I have the urge to close my eyes and fall forward to see if Eric would catch me, because I think he would. "Just tell me the truth," I say. "Did you really live with a foster family?"

"Three."

"What happened?"

"Not much," he says with a shrug. "I grew up. I just never knew my birth mother."

I shouldn't talk to him anymore—not if I really want him to leave—but I can't help it. "So why don't you find your birth mother? I mean, that would probably make a great *documentary*. People love that kind of stuff. Why don't you find her instead of me? If you don't mind my asking."

"No, you're entitled. But, see, I did find her. It took me a bunch of years, but I finally found her."

"She was alive?"

"Yup."

"Wow. That's amazing."

"In a way," he says quietly.

"So you had this, like, this big, tearful reunion?"

"No. Nope, just the opposite," he says. "She did cry at first, but then she said, 'You're a complete stranger to me. Why'd you have to go digging into my life?!' *Her life*, you know? I had nothing to do with it. I was irrelevant to her life. She hadn't wondered about me enough to actually want to find me. She didn't have a bundle of unsent letters to me tied up in a blue ribbon, you know, like the orphaned kid finds in the movie version."

"I'm sorry."

"No, no, it's no big deal—it's why I'm here, I guess. It's sort of why I first became interested in you. Because there you were…a kid whose mother's existence seemed to completely depend on her. Abbie Handler, the most loved kid," he says, without the slightest hint of irony.

"Oh, no," I say, choking back the urge to cry. "You're wrong. You can see now that you're wrong."

"Well, at the time I couldn't. I actually read *Girls' Guide*—the first one—when I was a kid. I remember—I was with foster mom number two, and she was, if you can believe it, a fan of your mother's." He seems to be genuinely embarrassed by this confession. "It was the only reading material in the house besides a book by Marianne Williamson and a lot of back issues of *People*. I remember her bringing it into the bathroom after coffee. She'd be in there a long time, and sometimes I'd hear her laugh out loud. I'd run in when she was through, and I'd find your mother's book open on the edge of the tub. I read it cover to cover. Twice. I started dreaming about the girl in the book...you. I knew enough, not being the center of anyone's world, to know there was this girl who was the *core* of a mother's universe. A girl, I figured, whose life must be, you know—perfect. I was invisible and you were the opposite. Your life was cherished and witnessed and recorded, and mine was...well, not that it matters, it was fine. But it wasn't *that*."

"Eric, that's so sad. Listen, I'm sure my life seemed like a party compared to yours. I don't even know what to say—"

"No, it's okay...really. Like, everything for a reason, you know? No big deal. But you stuck with me—I guess you sounded really interesting. I would read your mother's blog every so often—I stumbled on it a few years back. Then you disappeared from it, and I started wondering what was going on with you—which is how I came up with the idea for the documentary. You're right, I guess there's a pattern to my...choice of subjects," he says with a little laugh. "But I understand now why you'd want it, you know, the attention, to end. The Leung sisters, Sonia McQueen—I mean, if that's who she really is, because I'm not stupid—they're all pretty crazy in their own way, you know. But you're not crazy."

"No, I'm not," I say, feeling like it's the last stop on a bus and one of us is about to get off. "You're a little disappointed, aren't you? You're one of those guys who *likes* 'crazy'—who's into rescuing crazy girls."

"No, no, I don't do that."

"Yeah, I bet you do," I say, feeling now like I want to shove him off the bus, or at least goad him into leaving. "Bet your M.O. is dating crazy girls with eating disorders and psychotic mothers—girls who you can play daddy to. But I don't need a daddy, and I don't spend all day counting fat grams obsessively, and I don't do email in all lowercase."

Eric stands in front of me, not blinking. *Go ahead, I'll outstare you, and you can run for the door.*

"In that case," he says, "I'm *not* interested in you."

"Good," I say.

"Good," he echoes.

"Cool."

"Yeah, now that I've met you, I think the documentary would just get in the way."

"Right," I say automatically. Wait a minute—*get in the way*? Eric reaches out and lightly brushes the hair out of my face with his middle finger and tucks it behind my ear. Then he leans into that ear and whispers, his lips grazing my earlobe, his breath warm and ticklish. "I'm...*not*... because of you... if that's okay," he whispers playfully, but my brain is shouting so loudly that I miss pieces of the sentence. Or maybe that's all he said: "I'm...*not*...because of you." That's okay—that's enough.

He steps back, a broad smile on his face. "I've never said that before."

What?! My heart feels like a racquetball playing too hard against my chest. *Oh, God.* I feel panicked, like I've missed the last words of a dying person. I nod, hoping that will let Eric know I don't want him to leave.

"I'll stick around for a while," he says. "Whatever you need or want me to do, I'll do. But you know what's ironic?"

"No." I fill my lungs with air. "But I'm sure you'll tell me."

"I wouldn't be here if it wasn't for Ruth."

I look off into the shadows, then sit on the ground and wrap my arms around my knees. "I think I need a little alone time."

Eric retreats into the house. I turn and watch him through the porch doors, moving easily among the others, then taking a place on the footstool next to Winnie and Anthony. They create a strange tableau, Eric and the Gang of Five. If my mother was observing this same scene with me, and I was five, she might say: "Look, Abbie—it's after-hours in the people zoo, and here's a family of humans in Tucson, in their natural stone-and-glass habitat. Look, Abbie, look at their sweet faces. Look at the beautiful boy cub." She would think that up to tell me.

Something hard and flat tugs at my back pocket—the little notebook from my grandmother's bra. I yank it out and pull a lantern over for a better look. It could be a dozen years old. The cardboard covers have been bent and straightened so many times that they're like suede. Written in Esther's handwriting on the front is "Know This."

January 15, it reads on the first page, but what year? It's written in my grandmother's long, angular handwriting, like the results of a lie-detector test gone mad. The lines are fairly straight up and down but with a tiny break in the downward stroke of the J and the 5. On the last page with writing, about three-quarters of the way through the notebook, is the word *Yesterday.* That's what it's titled—the lines shaky, the first Y looking more like a U too tall to fit, the last Y tucked halfway under the A. It could have been written by a seven-year-old, by a drunk, or by Esther earlier this year.

January 15: Today Max would have been forty-one. He was such a beautiful boy. I wonder whether he would have kept his hair. It was very thick and curly, so he didn't get it from my side, since my hair has always been straight and thin. Ruth is a very wonderful girl. She's not a girl though, she keeps reminding me. Abbie is the girl. Beautiful Abbie. Ruth loves her so much that I worry that she will grow sick from some sadness disease when the day comes that Abbie leaves home. All diseases come from sadness, don't they? Ask Justin. He would know.

New Year's Day
Resolutions:
Tell Abbie.
Tell Abbie not to blame Ruth.
Tell Ruth not to blame Abbie.

The last entries are in fragments—letters written backward, words crossed out with such force that I can trace the Xs like Braille. Ruth as me, me as Ruth. *"Ruth came to visit today. She is eighteen next month."* Then "Ruth" crossed out and my name written above it. Me as Ruth, Ruth as me. I guess it doesn't really matter. I'm whoever Grandma wants me to be, because she has an illness that's eating her memory. I wonder if I ripped out certain pages in the book, all the sad and painful stuff, and then gave it back to her, would she know the difference? Maybe that would give her some peace. The same thing might work if I rewrote my diary. Then, one day, years from now, when my own memory is failing, I could pick it up and reread it and remember my mother however I wanted. But that would be cheating.

twenty-one

RUTH

ey!" Another car speeds by, only the third in fifteen minutes—this one passing close enough to break the well of tears in my eyes and pull the spit out of my mouth. "Fuck!" The tears and spit on my cheeks run across my face like driving rain on a windshield. "You fucking amoeba! Stop!"

I can't yell anymore.

There's no one to hear me, and there are no lights except from the windows of the few low buildings in the distance. I'm sweating the kind of sweat induced by fear and nerves, which always reeks sour and stale—the kind of sweat that's immediate and starts behind your neck after you've narrowly avoided accidental death. The road ahead inclines underneath blackness, dipping up, then down in gentle waves. I know this only because the taillights of the car that just whipped by disappear and reappear, like an alien ship making an uncertain landing, glancing off the ground, then moving forward for another attempt, over and over. Jesus, I'll hyperventilate if I keep crying this hard. Must stop. I've got to push the urge to cry back into my throat, trap the sobs, keep from coming apart. "Fuck! Somebody! Come on!"

"Fug, Gumbogy! Gubbon!" It sounds like I'm drowning. Like the way I cried out in my dreams after Missy disappeared. It was always the same dream: me in a meat locker surrounded by mutilated bodies, slipping around in a puddle of blood yelling for help, trying to scream, but only managing garbled cries.

"FUG! GUMBOGY! GUBBON!" I scream again.

Another car passes so quickly that it parts my hair to the opposite side.

"FOGGGUG!" I am a pathetic, bleating *figgeroga. Fog gathby bleat me scrobberaba in the bloody desert. Trove the borogoves. Trove the borogoves.* I am the Jabberwocky. Missy loved that poem. She said it gave her hope, not understanding it, but loving the way it sounded. Not understanding the thing you love, but loving it fiercely anyway—because what difference does it make if you don't know what a borogove is? I used to recite that poem to Abbie when she was a little girl. She'd turn her eyes upward. "I'm watching the words dance on the ceiling," she'd tell me.

A light from another car shines at my back, but this one doesn't pass by—it slows down, this one, which scares me more than a speeding semi. Oh, Jesus, it's *following* me. Car, go. Go car! Car, don't kill me. Car, don't be driven by a recently jilted teenage boy who's decided to go hunting for women with his father's high-powered rifle. I feel like I'm going to throw up. The car's caught up with me, and I still don't turn. I feel the heat of the engine on my back, but for some reason I think I'll be safer if I don't turn my head and look. The passenger window slides open. *Shhhhhh*, it warns, until it detracts altogether with a final *thmmp*.

I'm ready to take flight when…

"Ruthie," the driver says.

"Gaugh! Damn! Justin, you scared me!"

Alongside me now, Justin watches amusedly as I knead a kink in my side and an ache in my back from running in sandals down the highway. I've just enough energy left to walk around to the passenger side and collapse in the seat.

"Where were you going?" he says, handing me the bottle of water that seems to have simply appeared in his hand. "Don't gulp it."

I can't gulp it because my body is trying too hard to expel liquids at this moment. I feel like I've peed my pants, but that must be sweat—sweat and more mucous. How is it possible that I have enough liquid left in my body for the tears that keep rolling out of my eyes and into my mouth?

"I'm cold," I say, shivering.

Justin turns on the heat, then pulls off the road past the gravel shoulder into a shallow drainage ditch and parks, the front of his truck forty-five degrees lower than the back. We sit there, suspended, like at the top of the roller coaster at Great Adventures. I hold my breath, imagining that at any moment we could drop down and begin the best part of the ride, which always meant the beginning of the end. The best rides never last long enough—I stopped loving amusement park rides soon after I realized that—so why bother going on them in the first place? Although I never did figure out what "long enough" might be.

The silence between us doesn't feel the least bit awkward. I could sit in it for hours, close my eyes and imagine the drone of the heater as crashing waves, the warmth as a painless and insidious vapor gradually creeping in and erasing my memory. "I feel…completely hollow."

"That's good," Justin says.

It surprises me to laugh, and doing so instantly clears the mucous from my throat. "Jesus, Justin. Fuck you." I start crying again, then giggle uncontrollably until I can finally hold up my hand. "T.O."

"No, really, that's good," he says, reassuringly. "You can't fill a vessel until it's completely empty."

"My head hurts. My Xanax is gone. I feel like I'm having an aneurysm."

"Stop for a minute. Just stop everything, Ruth."

"Would you be able to tell? Could you tell if I was having an aneurysm? Does your mind go blank right before?"

"Give me your hand," Justin says, but he doesn't wait for me to offer it.

"Oh, I hate that," I say as Justin taps the fleshiest part of my hand, above my thumb joint, slowly and steadily applying more pressure. I brace myself, squeezing my butt tightly so I don't cry out as his oversized thumb threatens to separate my carpal bones. But the pain in my right temple is greater than the anticipation of pain from my hand. He kneads and kneads, and not until I look down do I realize that he has grasped my left forearm with his other hand

and is pressing into the skin so my flesh squeezes through between his fingers. The stabbing in my temple turns into a throb, first red, then yellow, then white behind my closed eyes. Justin breathes in through his nose, out with a haaaaaaaa through his mouth…now, words, hummed in unintelligible cadences. A mantra…an antidote…a prayer. His kindness makes me so fucking angry that I don't know how to respond. My hand doesn't budge when I send it the signal to move. My mother is in the same predicament, but her lack of bodily response is due to a stroke. Could I be having a stroke right now? Yes, sure, that's a possibility—my brain has finally blown and paralyzed my left side. I'll try to speak.

"N-no, stop, Justin. I can't—"

"Shut up, Ruth. Just be quiet. Please. For once."

For once. Yes. He kneads the pain out of my head, kneads until I can't hear my own breath—until his hands melt through my skin like molten lava over rock.

Something takes shapes in the distance as he presses and rubs—something with small, blinking yellow lights moving very, very slowly toward us, parallel to the road—not a car or machine. It bumps slightly up and down in rhythm. Up, down, up, down. Now that it's closer, I can make out a string of lights in a U around it. I'm watching it sideways, because my head is resting on Justin's shoulder. No, wait—it's a man riding a horse, which is adorned with a blinking necklace of Christmas lights. I can hear the languid slap of hooves on the ground and make out the figure in the saddle. The rider is old, with a short gray beard, gold wool skull cap, and brown bomber jacket, the twinkling lights reflecting off a spur on one boot. He passes on my side, seeming oblivious of the car. When he's in line with me, he turns his head and smiles, nodding. I nod back. He's missing part of a leg.

"Justin, that man had one leg."

"I saw."

"My head is better."

"I know."

"I don't know how to do anything else," I say, after sucking in and exhaling enough air to inflate a small life raft. "That's so depressing."

"You know how to make sour-cream apple pie from scratch."

"I do know that. It's too late to learn anything else, like chemistry, or science, or medicine, or something like that—isn't it? I could become a paramedic if I wanted to. I've always wanted to do that. Abbie would appreciate it. Especially if I tended to head trauma. I hate blood—but I could do that."

"You could do that."

"You did see the one-legged man, didn't you?"

"In a bomber jacket and blinking lights."

"Good. Good." I haven't been this close to Justin for this long in years. "One true thing about me," I say to him. "Just tell me one, without thinking—off the top of your head."

"You. Anticipate. Grief," he answers immediately and slowly, so as to keep the one true thing suspended between us for as long as possible. "No, let me revise that: You mourn the loss of everything prematurely. You assume everyone will eventually leave you, so you act the way you do…"

"You mean badly."

"And then, when they do leave, you act like 'Good. Go. I knew it. Leave. I don't care.'"

"How long have I been doing that?"

"For as long as I've known you. You even anticipated Abbie leaving home from the moment she could walk. And you couldn't stand that thought. Ever."

"If that's true, I must be…very fucked up."

"Not more than most people," he says, matter-of-factly.

"Does Abbie hate me?"

"Not at all."

I'm no longer sure I can believe this. "Have *you* ever hated me?" I ask, but I already know the answer.

"I have."

"Well, I've hated *you*."

"I know."

"Do you know when I hated you?"

"I think so," he says.

"I hated you when you gave up your Marlboros. I hated you when you gave up journalism. I hated you when you graduated from all your acupuncture and meditation and hoo-ha training. I hated you for being in all the family photos when I wasn't, because I was too busy taking them. And, you know, I especially hated you when you stopped getting angry. I hated that especially."

"I never stopped getting angry, Ruth."

"Oh!" I say, genuinely surprised. "Well, now I feel really stupid."

"You should."

"When did you hate *me*?"

Justin's lips press tightly together as if trying to keep one of those speckled fairy-tale toads from popping out. "When?" I insist.

"When you became Ruth Sternberg dot com," he says evenly.

"What?! Is this a conspiracy or something? I *am* that person. I write about me, my life. That *is* me."

"It wasn't always. You became her. And then nobody's secrets were safe. Nobody could have a private moment around you, Ruth. Everything about everybody became fair game."

I start to cry again. "I never told about my mother. I promised myself I wouldn't. I promised, and I keep my promises."

"What about Abbie?"

"What? Abbie is my child. I'm allowed to write about her because I love her and she was part of me...*is* part of me. Every moment of every day, whether she's with me or not. You don't understand that. And it made her strong. That's why she's so strong. I didn't burden her with all my shit, the way some people do with their kids—all that back story about family tragedies and long-lost friends. Besides, all daughters think their mothers are crazy at some point, so it doesn't matter."

"I swear, Ruth, if I didn't believe otherwise, I'd say you *were* crazy. And trust me, I know how you feel about that word. You need to tell Abbie everything. You need to fill in the gaps. Let her handle it for herself."

"My mother..."

"Esther doesn't care anymore. She doesn't want to hold

on to any secrets. If anything, she needs to let them go now—to lighten her load so that she can leave in *peace*, Ruth."

The one-legged cowboy has disappeared beyond the taillights. If this were a fable, it would tell how the moon is pulled into the sky by an old man on a horse who sacrificed his leg for one glorious full moon every thirty days. The old man would appear to only one person on his lonely path, leaving that person to question her sight and reason. I'd be that person in the story, and Justin could be the enchanted Joshua tree that sprang from the heart of a felled warrior... or maybe the Joshua tree that topples in my moment of epiphany, killing me instantly.

Justin is driving excruciatingly slowly back to Abbie's house, but it's all right, because I'm in no hurry. "Okay, tell her everything," I say, but I'm dubious. "Any...questions, comments, or additions?" Justin manages a tight smile. "Remember Abbie's third-grade teacher, Mrs...Kray? Krueger? She used to ask that question after show and tell: 'Any questions, comments, or additions?' Remember? I'd quiz Abbie before she went to bed on what the other kids might come up with. I'd pretend I was snotty David Kruplitz asking his obnoxious questions just so Abbie would be prepared. I wanted her to be prepared."

"She was."

"She was what?"

"Prepared. You did a good job of preparing her."

"Thanks."

"You're welcome."

"I've never lied to you, Justin."

"I know that," he says. "But maybe you should have. On a few occasions."

Justin stops the car a short distance from Abbie's house and kills the lights. Parked at a post in front of the house is the horse with the twinkle lights. My daughter's elderly friends move back and forth in the window, Abbie doing double time among them. After a couple of minutes, the front door swings open, belching out two of the women, the old man named Anthony, and my one-legged horseman with a cane, who gestures to his animal. I roll down my window to try to take in what they're saying. "Abbie will hold onto"—I can't make out the name—"*Tonto*?" says one of the women, as they both gently usher the horseman toward one of the cars. Abbie stands in the doorway waving goodbye as they pile in and drive off.

"I have to be back in town by morning, Ruth," Justin says. "I can't cancel this client. He's had terrible trauma."

I start to laugh, and Justin smiles knowingly. *Like I'm not in trauma*, my laugh says. *I'm sure that you feel you're in trauma*, Justin's mouth, curled at the corners, implies.

"Anyway," he says, "I do have to get back tonight."

"I think…I think I'll stay. Either that or I'll find a lift to the airport. Or Harry will come back. Or Mom will—um, no. Or something."

"Whatever's supposed to happen will. But say goodbye to Abbie for me, and tell her I'll call her tomorrow."

I nod and kiss him on the side of his head. Justin doesn't look at me as I slide out of his truck, even though I wait to catch his eye before shutting the door. I watch him circle around and head off down the highway, his taillights disappearing so quickly that I can only assume he was beamed up to the mothership.

I'm not ready to go in yet, even though the howling in the distance isn't distant enough for me; three or four coyotes, it sounds like…maybe a whole clan. Dogs in the neighborhood answer back, only making their wild cousins scream louder. The coyotes are probably in a cave, sharing a kitty cat grabbed from someone's yard—a cave littered with little kitty-cat collars from past supper orgies. It's one thing listening to the coyotes in L.A. from the comfort of your own bedroom, another thing altogether when your only protection is the night air. The yipping revs up as I move toward the house. I'm not going to run, I'm going to calmly walk back to the house—especially since I see Abbie in the window, looking right at me. I am calm and graceful. But I go to take a jaunty little leap in the direction of the house and trip over a half-buried brick in the dirt. It's one of those stupid falls that you hear about people— usually old ones—taking on a leisurely stroll, and they wind up sprawled on the sidewalk. So here I am, sprawled on the gravel. *Oh, Ow!* My hands and knees sting from breaking my fall. My forehead's the last to hit, almost an afterthought—kissing the ground without enough force to cause any real damage, but enough to make for a shower of tiny pebbles down my face when I raise my head. I lick my bleeding, stinging palms, then pull myself to a sitting position. I wait a moment, then look up at the window and see that Abbie is gone—rather, she's right here beside me, draping a blanket over my shoulders. Strange, the howling has ceased.

"Are you all right? Ruth? Are you—" Abbie says, as she drops cross-legged on the ground next to me. "Um…Ruth, I—" she tries to finish, but she's having trouble keeping a straight face. "Oh, my gosh, I'm sorry. Are you all right?" She laughs, unable to quell the giggles. God, I love her laugh, even now—it breaks apart and dances around me, tickling me behind my ears, coaxing me to play.

"Oh, sure," I say, feeling a bit drugged. "Laugh, clown, laugh."

The loudest peal yet erupts, followed by quiet. "Oh. Ruth," Abbie says, the pity in her voice apparent. "You—you would not believe what you looked like when you fell…or what you look like now. Are you okay?"

"I am *not* okay."

Abbie looks at my foot, which is twisted uncomfortably inward, and frowns.

"But I'm not hurt," I add quickly. She puts her hand on my ankle. "Don't! Don't touch!" I warn her only because I can't bear her light, tender touch. I want it, but I can't bear it. "I've got to tell you…some…stuff."

Her face goes slack. It's telling me, *Nothing you can say will ever surprise me. I know exactly how you're going to explain yourself, and it won't affect me in the least. Never does.*

So I decide to start with the facts.

"I was eight. Max was five."

"Max? Who is Max?"

"Max was my little brother."

"What are you talking about?"

"Grandma didn't want you to know. She was afraid—"

"You tell me, Ruth. You stay right here and you tell me.

I don't care if we sit here all night," my daughter says, sounding exactly like...me.

"We lived in Jackson Heights," I say. "Queens. Before we moved to Long Island. Grandma had her own business. She sold beauty products from this little storefront that smelled like jasmine—with tea, and fresh brewed coffee, and honey cake for all her lady shoppers. There were always fresh flowers. She loved that store. It was her sanctuary."

"How come she never talked about it? I asked you once if—"

"Give me a chance, Abbie. Please. Max and I spent Saturday afternoons at Mom's store. Playing around. There was a toy store across the street," I say in a monotone, hoping not to relive the story. I continue quickly—just the facts. "I was allowed to cross the street. Max wasn't. Mom told Max not to leave the store, and I told Max not to leave the store. I was going to buy something for him. I had three dollars in my purse—this crocheted purse on a braided string I had. Isn't that crazy? The things we remember..." Abbie's eyes are wide, her hands over her mouth. "Esther used to say that Max belonged to me. Max talked to people through me...and I was his translator, whispering into his ear, even if I was just repeating what someone had said to him. Max liked anything I liked. He liked those goofy faces that you move the black metal shavings over with a magnet to make mustaches and hairdos. He liked colored pencils. I was going to the store to buy him new ones. I told him to stay put. And he didn't." My eyes start to well up, so I talk faster. "It was raining and the traffic was heavy...and the cab dragged him underneath its wheels all the way down the street, until it stopped at the light. I got to him first."

I can't risk looking at Abbie until I finish, because I can't bear to see the look on her face. "After the funeral, Mom took to her room for a week. I never even saw her come out to use the bathroom. My father brought trays of food in and out. My aunt Joanne—Mom's older sister—came to stay with us. She took me to matinees and lunches at the Horn & Hardart, but I don't remember us ever talking. No one talked about Max being dead. My father actually said to me, 'Ruthie, we're not going talk about this any more. It's all over, and it'll just make everyone feel bad all over again. It's private. Do you understand? If you talk about it, it'll just be like it's happening all over again. And you don't want that, do you? You don't want to make it happen all over again.' Like I had the power to do that, just by mentioning it. So, when my mother finally came out of her room, we all acted like everything was all right, like nothing bad had ever happened. Max's belongings were boxed and stored, and it was like everyone was playing the same game of Let's Pretend. If we bumped into someone at the market or on the street who happened to mention Max, my mother would speak fondly of him but with this total detachment, like Max was some uncle who died at the ripe old age of ninety after a lifetime of fun living. 'Max, yes,' she'd say, with this zombielike smile, 'we all certainly miss him.'"

Abbie inhales sharply, startling me. Lost in remembering the words to a story that is nearly forty years old and told only twice before—once for Missy, then to Justin—I'd nearly forgotten she was here.

"Your grandfather didn't handle it any better than Mom, if that's possible. He…he was a failed writer, did you know? A failed writer working to support his little family by writing ads for the local pennysaver. He'd come up with these flowery ads that sounded like they were from some turn-of-the-century romance novel. After Mom decided to come out of the bedroom, he just disappeared. Literally. *For seven weeks.* Not a word to me, nothing. It was as though the two of them had made some arrangement to take turns with their grief. My mother actually told me that he was on sabbatical. That was the word she used—*sabbatical*. Can you believe it? I had to look it up. I thought it was a place that people went after their kid died. Then, one day, he reappeared—joined us at the breakfast table one Sunday morning, said hello to me, kissed me on the cheek, and asked me whether or not I wanted sturgeon on my bagel."

Abbie is silent. This is the longest I've spoken uninterrupted to her since she left home.

Where was I? Oh, yeah, sturgeon. Abbie and I stare intently out at the same nothing. I remember staring like this at the living room ceiling of my parents' apartment. It had started to crack after my father returned. There was this high-rise going up at the end of our block, and we could register the pounding by how the orange juice shimmied in our breakfast glasses. Small hairline cracks—not even cracks, just long dark lines—began appearing where the

ceiling met the walls. Within a couple months, the lines
began opening up, spreading wider and wider until some of
the separations were nearly half an inch wide. My parents
seemed oblivious to the cracks, but I was obsessed with
them, as if they held Max's absence—and I was sure that it
was only a matter of time before they'd be the cause of the
whole building collapsing around us.

"About six months after Max died, when I thought
things couldn't get any weirder, I realized that Esther
was…*shrinking*. I hadn't noticed anything different about
her eating habits, just that her clothes were getting looser,
and the skin on her arms and face. I knew something was
wrong, but I didn't know what, and I didn't know what to
say. Then, when Mom decided to host Thanksgiving for
the first time ever, I should have known that something
bad was going to happen. Mom had never attempted
Thanksgiving dinner for our family, let alone for her two
sisters' families. Mom and Dad and Max and I always went
out to dinner, or upstate to your grandfather's sister's house
in Schenectady.

"At first, I was kind of excited about having Thanksgiving at our house. Until I saw the turkey, you know—Esther
wanted a *freshly killed* bird—headless and raw. It was the
first time I'd ever seen one before, that big and dead. It was
plucked, and very cold, and the skin reminded me of what
was left on Mom's shrunken arms, so there was no way I
was going to eat it.

"After a pretty normal if not unnaturally quiet dinner,
we're all sitting around the table ready for dessert. Mom
announces that she'll be right back, and then she trots off

to the bathroom. We're all waiting, all nine of us, imagining what?—apple pie with ice cream, right? Next thing we know, Esther is dragging this big, heavy doctor's scale from the bathroom along the wood floor. Drags it into the dining room—bumping, scratching—the thing dinging up the floor, 'cause it's like a hundred pounds and almost the size of her. She's sweating and grunting, and she hauls the thing over to the table with this crazy smile on her face. My dad says something, but no one else does. Mom kicks her chair out of the way and sets up the scale. She jumps on it and says—I remember it exactly—she says, 'Now, let's see if I really do exist! I've been shrinking, you know? And I thought it'd be nice if you could…validate—is that the word I'm looking for, honey?' she says to me—'*validate* that I'm still here.' She flicks the weight thingie with her finger, trying to balance the scales, then she starts yelling, 'Shit! I should have had some *pie* first! Pie would make a *huge* difference.'"

"What was everyone else *doing*?" Abbie asks.

"Nothing! I mean, the grown-ups were doing nothing. They were *supposed* to do something, but we were all just watching Mom. Finally, Aunt Kitty stands up and goes to Mom, but Mom grabs this leftover leg from the turkey platter. She holds it like a club, yelling something about—I can't remember. And the cousins start to cry, and finally, *finally* my father and Kitty try to coax Mom out of the room. He's whispering in her ear, and Kitty's whispering, too, and then Esther goes ballistic. She runs back to the table, grabs the apple pie, and hurls it against the dining room wall. Kitty takes me and the cousins outside—I don't know how they got her to stop. And the next morning, Mom was gone. For four weeks. My father said to me, 'Your mother's having some difficulty. Let's not make a mountain out of a molehill.' And that was it—that's all he would say. So Mom was gone, and we start a new game called 'Mom's gone crazy and we don't know when she'll be back.' And while she was gone, I kept finding little chunks of the apple pie—stuck to the molding, encrusted in the carpet, petrified on a light bulb. I'd point out the pieces to my father, because it was the only way I could relive Thanksgiving—you know, indirectly, without referring to the actual incident. 'Dad,' I'd say, 'I found a piece on the bookshelf today.' I'd bring him in the living room and point. He'd nod and wipe it off. Not a word."

I pause. "Mom came home from her *vacation* just before Christmas."

"Grandma must have said *something*," says Abbie, my logical, practical, empathetic daughter. "She must've said something when she came back. What did she say?"

"She said—on the day your grandmother returned home—she said, 'Hello, cookie, you're looking very grown up.' That's what she said."

"Is that when you moved? Is that why you all moved?"

"Yeah. Forty miles east, a world away—people in Queens don't think that the rest of Long Island is even *in* New York—to the house I showed you that time we went back. Not a trace of Max left over. We left all the trauma behind."

Abbie propels herself to her feet and moves a few steps

away. She raises her hands to her face, then wipes the backs of her hands on her pants.

Funny, I never reminisce on my Max-less childhood home in the suburbs—the suburbs of Long Island, the last stop of migration from Brooklyn, Queens, and the Bronx. We went east, to the promised land, to the grids of manicured lawns in front of one-family homes on cul-de-sacs, dead ends, and landfills, leaving behind the people who knew us when Max was alive, to the place where people didn't have breakdowns. Instead, they rusted from the outside in, in a process that took years. Our new home looked the same as the ones on either side of it, with its avocado-green appliances, indoor-outdoor kitchen carpet, playroom, spare bedroom, basement, two and a half baths, and no room for the memory of Max or my mother's post-Thanksgiving weigh-in. The house to our left even had the same mimosa tree in front as ours. A few years later, it was discovered that the husband in that house had been having an ongoing affair with a fifteen-year-old babysitter while his kids played intramural sports, which came out after the babysitter tried to kill his wife. The house to the right, where my schoolmate Tara lived, had the same avocado-green appliances but no furniture, because Tara's father had gone bankrupt and left the family without a dime.

Meanwhile, my mother went to work at the cosmetics counter at Macy's. She found some happiness working long hours, painting new metallic faces on hopeful suburban housewives (blue shadow has *never* been out of style, according to Esther).

And as long as I'm leaking like a sieve, I tell Abbie that
I eventually found refuge in a small notebook that I carried
everywhere, and I found happiness in a best friend named
Missy, which is how I survived. It's not an excuse, it's just
the truth. Missy will tell you herself, I say, because now
she's found me, and she's the only other person I know who
remembers.

twenty-two

ABBIE

I wondered about that friend you kept coming back to on your blog."

Ruth looks surprised that I've been following her these last eight months. How can that surprise her? Even though it's kind of touching that it does. "I've got to keep tabs on you somehow," I offer.

"Yeah?" she says, obviously pleased, hoping, I can tell, for another sign of encouragement. "But that stuff about Max—and about Grandma losing her mind," I say instead. "I'm surprised you didn't wind up with *cancer*." My mother winces. "You know, people get cancer for keeping in less than that."

"Esther never wanted you to know. You know how private she is."

"So Grandma made you promise that you wouldn't tell anyone?"

"She...she didn't have to. But when she realized that she's going to die, she—it's like she became fearless. She told me that I might need to tell you...that I should tell you one day if it would 'help.' I hate asking for help."

"So is it helping?" I ask.

My mother looks away for a few moments. "She never talked about Max again. Esther came *undone*, is what people called it, because of what happened, because of all the things she never said aloud. *Undone*—like her shoelaces became untied, you know? She went *crazy*, Abbie. Nobody would even *say* the word back then, but the whole thing drove her crazy. I wasn't going to let that happen to me."

"So to keep that from happening, you decided to say everything out loud. Is that it?"

"Uh-huh," says Ruth, nodding. "Open book. Everything out in the open. Almost."

"Oh, my God, Mom...talk about *crazy*."

My mother remains silent.

"I'm sorry about Max, and about Missy. That must've been awful. You must've been sad for a long time."

"I was. It happened to me twice. But then you came along, and I loved you more than either of them—which I never would have believed was possible. More than everyone. Too much. It was like my whole world was this helium balloon that could explode or fly away...and *I* would come *undone*."

Ruth sits sniffling, wiping her nose with her sleeve, pursing her lips to keep them from quivering.

"I'm glad you're telling me this, Mom. But that doesn't mean I can forget everything. I'm not going to forget how angry I am at you just because…because you…look so pathetic sitting here with a pebble embedded in your forehead." I want to laugh, but I'm not letting her off the hook just yet.

"Oh, dear, I do? Oh, dear. In my forehead?" Ruth says, without making an attempt to wipe away the pebble or fix her hair.

Oh, dear? Oh, dear? Who is this person who isn't spewing mouthfuls of obscenities at the pebbles? I reach out and smooth her hair from her forehead. Her eyes well up. I brush the stone away, brush the hair at her temple. It's changed, the texture of her hair—it's coarser and lighter than I remember, like threads unraveled from an old cotton shirt. When I was little and my mother would lean over me in my bed, thinking I was asleep, her long, smooth hair would graze my face. It felt like the silk fringe on one of Grandma's scarves. I never understood why she needed to look so closely at me when she thought I was sleeping. She'd brush my hair aside with one finger, turn off my nightlight and tiptoe out.

"You were perfect from the moment you opened your eyes," Ruth says, hoarsely. "A perfect baby—and then you were perfect because you didn't let *anything* get under your skin. That's what I thought. You never let on when things got under your skin, the way that everything got under mine. You didn't complain, so I didn't think I'd done anything for you to complain about. I wondered how you could be wired the way you were, especially coming from… coming from me, you know? How does that happen? You were always warm—you ran warmer than most people, kicking off your sheets and blankets, sleeping in just your underpants even when it was freezing. You were always warm and dewy, when I'd be cold and drawn and annoyed by the slightest drafts—still hauling out those stupid space heaters in May. I wanted to be like you. I wanted your skin and teeth and roundness and the way you had empathy for the world, the way you seemed untroubled by me—which wasn't the truth, was it? Seems the truth is that you were just tolerating me. I was being *tolerated*. That's what I can't forgive myself for not seeing."

"I'm not going to be that way with *my* daughter," I say, because I can't resist the urge to let the last bit of wind from her sails.

"How very wise and very cavalier of you," Ruth says wearily.

"You…I told you things, and you…I…" *Breathe.* "Lots of things—blah, blah, blah. And everything was fuel for you. You had to regurgitate everything I said. I was, seven? Seven. I was having trouble sleeping. I was having the same dream every night, and I whispered it in your ear when you were tucking me in, because I was too freaked out to even say it aloud. It took me weeks to tell you that dream. Weeks!"

"Huh!? I remember! Wasn't that the naked-tree people…no, you mean—"

"No, you listen. It was the dream about Mark Goldberg—he was in my class, remember? In the dream, he's lying in a big filing cabinet, naked and asleep, and I keep him in the cabinet so I can look at him. And every night for a month, I look at him in my dreams, naked in his cozy little drawer. I thought something was wrong with me for having that dream, because sometimes I would—"

"Yes! I remember. The details—you went into these amazing details about his penis—"

"Ruth!"

"That dream was such a sweet metaphor for your budding sexuali—"

"Ugh, stop!" I yell. "I know what you thought of it. I know how you loved it. I know what you wrote. I knew it and everyone else knew it, and Ms. Rousseau changed my seat because of it. *She moved me away to the other side of the classroom…away from Mark Goldberg*, for God's sake! You have any idea what that made me feel like?"

Ruth sits silent, confused. "What?! You never told me that. You never told me that she moved your seat."

"Why would I tell you? Huh? So you could write about it? So you could call her a prude or an old fart or something dumb like that? Fix it so that I'd never be able to return to the second grade? Yeah, I definitely should have told you. That would have helped make the situation more normal, all right."

My mother's chest collapses, and a small sound—a little puff of "Oh!"—escapes, barely reaching me. "Abbie. I'm so…I'm so…" She runs out of breath before she can finish. "Oh," she mouths.

Watching my mother, messy and deflated, with hairline smudges of blood on her knees and forehead, I can't help but wonder how bullfighters gauge whether they've put enough swords into their staggering adversary. "It was embarrassing to me…you embarrassed me. Majorly," I say, because it's the worst thing I can think to tell her. A minute passes before my mother says anything.

"I'm embarrassing. I am." So now it seems there's no need for me to bring up any of the hundred and fifty-seven other public embarrassments she's responsible for.

"Do I have blood on my forehead? There's something wet." She scratches her bloody knee, then uses the same fingers to scratch her bloody elbow, then her forehead, so I can't tell where the blood is coming from.

"Your knees are bleeding."

"Really? Oh, right. That'll teach me."

My mother seems oblivious to her skinned knees, her dirty hands, and the pebble indentation in pinkish purple on her forehead. She smiles—this completely benevolent, *unrecognizable* smile, looking like she could break into a chorus of "Do-Re-Mi," which totally catches me off guard and makes me bark-laugh.

"Are you okay, honey?" she asks with the same smile. "Are *you* okay?" Maybe this sudden calm of my mother's is a side effect of some new antidepressants, or a middle-aged return to cannabis. "I'm not *on* anything," she answers, reading my mind. "Truly, I'm not on anything. Truly madly deeply. That's still one of my favorite movies. It's a shame Anthony Minghella died so young. Do you think anyone will say that after I die? 'It's a shame about Ruth Sternberg Handler, isn't it? Didn't she write those wonderful stories? About her daughter, weren't they?' No, I don't think so. And what does it matter, right?"

"Mom?"

"Yes, honey?" I now have my mother's full, serene attention, and I want to hold it in silence as long as I can. "Mom." I repeat, then wait, testing to see how long she can keep herself from jumping into the quiet space. I count to myself, slowly. One-two-three-four-five-six-seven. "Mom, what were you waiting for? When were you planning on telling me all this? I mean, were you gonna wait until… until I was feeding you pabulum in some nursing home, tweezing the hairs out of your chin?"

"You would do that for me?" she says brightly, in a voice much higher than normal. "Oh, Abbie—what else do I need to tell you? What can I tell you that would make your life better or perfect or more resolved? What can I tell you so that you'll love me?"

"Don't do that, Mom. I love you. I've always loved you. I just didn't *like* you very much. And maybe it would have helped to know all of this a lot sooner. Maybe I would have understood you better."

"Honey, you either love someone or you don't. You don't need somebody to unpack all their old baggage and rifle through it in order to decide whether you love them or not. It shouldn't matter."

It sounds right, what she's saying. If my most brilliant calculus teacher Mr. Keeshnu had said the same thing, I would have written it down on a Post-it and pasted it to my mirror to reflect on every morning—but when my mother says it, it sounds like a challenge. "Shouldn't matter, but it does," is all I can muster. "Could you just say you're sorry maybe?"

"Yes, of course," she answers with great resolve. "Yes, I'm sorry. I'm deeply sorry that I had no idea what an asshole I

was. I'm sorry that I…disappointed you." Then my mother
reaches out and gently pulls a piece of my hair through
her fingers, then another piece, then—having made certain that I won't bite her hand off—she moves closer,
then closer still. I help out by not moving a millimeter,
by breathing as shallowly as I possibly can without falling
over. She puts her arm around my shoulder and drops her
head in the crook of my neck, where it used to fit when I
was six. Unbelievably, it fits even better now than it did
then. "I'm sorry I didn't see your hurt," she says to me. "I
just don't know how that happened."

Winnie appears in the dark a few feet ahead of us. "I didn't
want to interrupt," she whispers. "Am I?"

"No. No," my mother says, lifting her head.

"I think it's your cell phone, Ruth," Winnie says,
handing it over to her. "It's been ringing and ringing and,
well, we didn't want to answer it or bother you. But it's ringing again, and it sounds very insistent. I think it's starting
to get angry."

Winnie and I help Mom to her feet, brushing the rest
of the embedded pebbles from her knees. Ruth punches
the keys on her phone, then listens. "Oh…oh. Oh, no. Oh,
Jesus," she says. "Harry's been calling. It *was* a black widow."

"Oh, dear," says Winnie.

My mother relays the information as she listens to
Harry's messages. "No, wait—they *think* it was a black
widow. He's at the hospital. He was driving, and he started
to feel his skin swell up…he blew up…he made it to the hos-

pital. Then…he's saying he looks like a big square tomato." She shuts her mouth, pursing her lips together to keep from laughing, and sputters instead, making snorting noises through her nose before ending the spasm with a long sigh. "I've got to go there, Abbie. I don't think it's far, and he's pretty scared. I think he took a swing at one of the orderlies. Um, could I borrow your, uh…" She stops and makes a face at my ancient Jeep in the driveway. "Shit, that's not stick is it? I can't drive stick. I mean, I could if I had to, but…"

"Why don't I come with you?" I say, automatically. "I'll drive. I can take you."

"Really? You could, really? But Esther won't have anyone—"

"Oh, silly," Winnie interrupts, "don't worry for a moment about your mother. I'll be here. I will not leave Esther's side until you return. Not a thing to worry about at this end."

My mother looks from Winnie to me. "Right," I say. "It'll be fine, Mom. No one I trust more than Winnie. But— Eric? Where's Eric? What's with—"

"Eric!" Winnie gushes. "Oh, goodness! Eric and I have been finding out that we're just two peas in a pod. He doesn't have any place he needs to be. You go, both of you. Just come in and give Esther a kiss goodbye. Let her know she's leaving. Tsk—silly me, I mean let her know *you're* leaving. *She's* not leaving, of course, unless that's what His plan is. You Know Who, I mean."

Grandma is propped up in my bed, her skin the same exact shade as the cream-colored leather interior of her Chrysler Newport. Her eyes are closed, but a faint smile crossing her lips reminds me of the expression on her face in a game we used to play after school. "What am I thinking about?" she would ask, leaning against the kitchen counter, her eyes closed, arms crossed, smiling like she is now.

"What you're gonna make for dinner?" I'd say.

"No."

"What you're gonna get me for my birthday?"

"No."

"Pound cake fried in butter with chocolate dripped on top."

"How did you guess?" she'd say, then we'd head out to Gelson's for pound cake and an industrial-size bag of Hershey's Kisses. Back home, I'd unwrap the foils and toss each little chocolate into the double boiler, watching them all turn into a pot of sweet molten lava.

🖱   🖱   🖱

My mother takes Esther's hand. "Mom. Mom?" Esther opens her eyes and frowns. "Mom? It's Ruth. Do you know where you are?"

"In the desert, dear. Don't you?"

"We're going to stay here a couple days, Mom. That okay with you?"

"Fine by me. Desert. Beach. Both the same except… for water."

"Alrighty, Mom. So Abbie and I have to leave for a few

hours, and then we'll be back."

"Grandma, Winnie is going to stay with you."

"Good," says Grandma. "You're my girls." She closes her eyes. "I'm sorry, Ruth."

"Me, too," my mother whispers.

"Why? Why are you sorry, dear?" Grandma says, looking hurt.

"Just…because," my mother says. The three of us look off in different directions, like strangers lost in their daydreams at a bus stop. My mother takes Grandma's hand and pets the back of it—long, slow strokes starting at her fingertips. "Why is it, do you think," she says, examining Grandma's fingernails—which I just now realize have never looked so strong and healthy—"why is it that after you're forced to say goodbye to someone you love, you have to spend the rest of your life being reminded of how much that person meant to you?"

"Hmm," Grandma murmurs.

"They have to die or leave, and then you're reminded of how much you loved them. Which makes them more a part of your life, in some weird way, than if they were still there. Why is that?"

"Just supposed to…" Grandma answers, then runs out of steam.

"Mom?" my mother says.

"Mm-hm?"

"Are you…are you scared?"

"Oh, no, dear," my grandmother says hoarsely. "Not now. Not any more. Curious. A little…sad. Very—so tired. Tired."

"I love you, Mom," my mother whispers in Grandma's ear.

"I love you, Grandma."

"Me, too," she mouths. "I...you."

⁀ᵇ   ⁀ᵇ   ⁀ᵇ

I gently close the bedroom door after us. Eric's the first thing I see when I spin around—Eric sitting on the floor with his knees pulled up under his chin, watching me. "Hey," he says quietly.

"Hey," I say. He nods, and I nod back.

"Okay," Winnie chirps in approval—like she's just managed to bring two rival toddlers together in the sandbox, and neither one has thrown a rock at the other's head. Not that she needed to worry. I wouldn't have done anything other than stare at him until an earthquake happened to swallow up everyone around us.

In one continuous move, Winnie grabs Eric's hand and pulls him to his feet, then loops one arm firmly through mine, the other around my mother, and walks the two of us to the front door before my brain can put on the brakes. Then she pushes a piece of paper in my hand. "Directions," she says, "just in case. You drive carefully, and don't worry about a thing. You'll be back in time."

"In time?" my mother asks, frowning.

"In time, meaning 'before you know it,'" Eric offers from behind.

"Of course," Winnie says. "We'll hold down the fort! Everything will be all right."

My mother slides into the front seat of my Jeep. "Is there any place we can pick up some good pound cake on the way back?" she says. "Your grandmother would love that, don't you think?"

My heart kicks my throat in surprise. *How could she know what I was thinking?* But why wouldn't she know? Esther and Ruth, Ruth and Abbie, mother and daughter... same fabric, different pattern. I steal a look at my mother's profile. Her jaw line is losing some of its tautness—a long way from Grandma's, but on the same trajectory. Her hands on her lap—with those slim fingers and bony knuckles—could be mine, except that hers are covered with tiny crisscrosses, as though sewn with ultrafine thread pulled too tightly. I grab some cheap hand cream out of the glove compartment and hand it to her. She nods her thanks, then kneads a palmful of the stuff over the top of each hand, quickly at first, then slowly, pulling and pressing long after the cream is absorbed, the way Grandma would do with her Jergens. I'm more haphazard in my approach, only because I feel vain and silly applying it behind the steering wheel at a red light, but I've always been mesmerized by the way my mother does it.

"That's what I whispered to Esther before we left," my mother says. "I told her we'd pick up a nice pound cake."

"You scare me sometimes."

"Feeling's mutual."

Eric and Winnie stand arm in arm at the door, waving. It's almost as though Winnie and the others concocted a fertility potion and produced Eric—a little bit of Miguel, a dash of Anthony, a touch of Winnie, a soupçon of Selma, Claire ripping off the afterbirth with her teeth and fingernails. Voila! There he was.

"You should really…" my mother begins as I drive off. "I mean, I'd really love it if you'd come back and help me go through Esther's place at some point. It won't be too monumental a job, because she's been giving away most of her stuff for the last couple years. The only stuff she's never given away is anything with writing on it—notebooks, lists, bills. A lot to sift through, you know, because I'm thinking that she's written down a lot of things throughout the years. I don't know—stories…on the backs of envelopes, on index cards and scrap paper."

"No kidding," I say.

My mother narrows her eyes, trying to read my mind. "It'll take forever if I go it alone—and you know how private…" She trails off.

"Yeah. I know how private Grandma is. I know. I can do that. We'll do it together."

My mother settles into the seat, putting her feet up on the dashboard. At what age will she stop being able to do that, I wonder—placing her feet against the dashboard with her knees in front of her face?

"You don't mind?" she says. "My feet?"

"No, not at all. Hey, you know what?"

"What?"

"Why don't we road-trip it to visit Missy. You said she's in Arizona."

"Oh, my God, wouldn't that be—"

"Crazy," I offer. "Now *that* would be crazy, wouldn't it?"

"We could do that. You know…after this is all over."

"I could come with you. Funny. I mean ironic-funny, huh? That Missy's out here, in the desert, too."

"Yeah," my mother says, gazing out the window, "because she loved the ocean, you know? Who woulda thought?"

Desert. Beach. Both the same, except for the water.

twenty-three

ESTHER

I love love parties, but I hate saying goodbye. It's a silly thing—you know what I'm talking about—that awkward moment after parties, dinners, coffee, or a date, when you're not ready to make a new date, when you've said everything silly and important and necessary that you've wanted to say, but you feel obliged to keep talking. *So, Mister Whosee-whatsis, we should do this every month/ week/second Wednesday…So, tell so-and-so and their cousin Mo that I said hello…Let's keep in touch. Mwah! Let's do this again. Mwah! Don't be a stranger, take care! I'll call…you better call. Mwah! Mwah!*

Let me tell you, I'm so relieved that it's not *me* doing the grieving this time. It's too exhausting. I couldn't do it now. I don't have the energy any more. Actually, I never did have the energy—and grieving always seemed such a self-centered thing to do. At the very least it was something to be done in private, but maybe I was wrong. Maybe Ruth wouldn't have—I don't want to say "suffered," because that's too strong a word—wouldn't have been so obnoxious? No, that's not it. Ruthie's just a little overbearing at times. She's a tough cookie. And that's not a bad thing. Maybe she wouldn't have been so screwed up if I'd shared my feelings more with her. Ugh, listen to me. Feelings schmeelings.

It's not as confusing as everyone makes it out to be—life, I mean. Life is what it is. It's what you can touch, who you love, how nice you are to the Chatty Cathy checkout girl at the grocery store. Simple. Visualize, schmizualize—you do the best you can, and when you can't, there's a reason why, even if you don't understand it. And don't waste. It's never good to waste anything, because waste is unforgivable. On that note, I feel very badly now for having given my cancer medicine to my plants these last few months. It was very wasteful of me because the medicine's very expensive, I'm told. But I have to tell you, my plants never looked so wonderful and healthy, so I don't feel *too* guilty about it.

I'll tell you what: I do love this woman, Winnie, and this young man, Eric, and Miguel and the others. I would like to leave with them by my side because I know they care, and because I won't feel *obliged* to say goodbye to them. They don't need me to explain anything—they'll just do as I want. Winnie will hold my hand, and that sweet boy will push the hair out of my face, and Anthony will play my music, and they will all help me leave this party without having to worry about what to say. It's an awfully small room, but I'm sure we'll all be able to fit. Right now Winnie is sitting on the bed, and Eric is cross-legged on the floor.

They're talking. I want to hear what they're saying.

✍   ✍   ✍

"Esther's asleep," Winnie says. "Anthony says you've made the cocktail before?"

"Oh, totally. Anthony's a very cool guy. He thought Esther didn't have enough barbs here, but she's got everything she needs in her bag—more than enough, actually. It's best in, like, chocolate syrup or applesauce."

"Or ice cream."

"Pomegranate juice is good."

"Theoretically, we could do this any time," Winnie says. "Esther says she doesn't have any 'blanks' she needs to fill in, no big secrets left for the girls to find out about, if you know what I mean?"

"Yeah, definitely—like finding out your mother isn't really your mother, she's your aunt…or being told you have the gene for a rare blood disease that eventually destroys your flesh. Like, there's nothing left to tell them that they'll need to ensure their *survival*, you know?"

Yes, he's correct, that Eric. Such a smart boy.

"Can I tell you something, Winnie? I've had this dream for years, but only occasionally—it's like I have it when I move someplace new or I start some big new project. I'm always lost in the dream—in some crazy road labyrinth in some city that looks vaguely like New York, but supersized and futuristic. I'm alone in my car and I don't have my cell or any directions, and I'm freaking out. And just in that moment when I think I could actually die, I look over and there's this girl sitting next to me, and she's really calm, and suddenly I know I'll be all right. Even though I never see her face clearly, I know who she is. I can feel who she is. She's the girl from the book. She's Abbie. I've always known it. I don't need to tell her story."

"That's good, Eric, because it's time for our young lady to go back. She's got that scholarship—trying so hard not to show how excited she is about it. She's been hiding here, before she's done anything to hide from."

"I understand," Eric says, then smiles this very sexy smile. "Winnie, you've *assisted* before, haven't you? I bet you have. I bet you have a few times out here."

"Only when I'm asked to," she says, smiling back at him. "How could you tell?"

"Takes one to know one."

"I like your choice of words, Eric. *Assisted* is the way I always think of it. It's so...*helpful*-sounding. Might I ask if it was a loved one for you?"

"Oh, sure. I mean, sure, you can ask, but, no, not exactly a loved one—not the way people usually mean it."

"Not family, you mean."

"No, his name was Mr. Ellison. He was a shut-in I brought food to. A really sweet old guy, dying of some cancer. He'd been storing up pills for weeks, and he just wanted to go. He didn't have any family, only a couple of friends, and they were totally supportive. They chipped in and brought a bottle of good Scotch and a best-of CD by his favorite singer, Tony Bennett. And then he asked me to hold his hand..." Eric starts choking up. "Whoa. Sorry..."

"Oh, honey, that's all right. I completely understand. That's a wonderful thing you did. I'm still on the fence about what to tell Abbie and her mother. I don't want them, um—'freaking out,' right?"

"Yeah, I know what you mean. But it's a strong cocktail—it doesn't take long after the sleep part. And there's no reason for anyone to think that a seriously ill eighty-five-year-old woman succumbed to anything other than being on this planet for so long. Don't you think?"

"I do. I certainly do."

Of course! Now I remember why Max's hair was so red and curly. I told my husband it was because I had red hair when I was a child, from a grandparent in the Ukraine I never knew. But it was that young man from very long ago, the one who worked as a copy boy at the pennysaver. Trevor. He was so young, with all that thick, unruly red hair. Only twenty-one, is that possible? He was the son of an older friend of mine—Delores, that was her name—and he was celebrating his twenty-first birthday. That's right. Delores and me and Patsy Cornell were teasing him. I told Trevor that I'd buy him his first *legal* drink. I didn't mean it seriously, but he called me on it. A few days later, my husband had a couple of friends over to watch something on the television, and Trevor and I went to a place nearby called the Velvet Turtle. Yes. I went to the Velvet Turtle with a lovely redheaded boy named Trevor on his twenty-first birthday. He made me giggle. My husband was a kind man, but he never made me giggle—and he preferred the company of his men friends to mine. What was his best friend's name? Dave. That's right, my husband always preferred Dave's company. Dave was the only person who could make him laugh. And that was fine by me, because Trevor could make me giggle…among other things. It was Trevor who I went to meet, after those first drinks at the Velvet Turtle—all those times when my husband thought I was going to the seven-thirty show at the RKO Keith. What I did was take the subway five stops over to Sunnyside, to meet Trevor in a tiny little bar where no one knew us, tucked away on a side street off Queens Boulevard, and within half an hour I would age backward from forty to nineteen. As long as the two of us sat in that bar, in the smoky dark, and walked in the night to his tiny little apartment four blocks away, and kept only the lamp with the orange shade on, I could be nineteen again—until I got back home to my husband and my demanding little Ruthie. If I kept my shoulders back and my head tilted slightly a certain way, in the sepia of the lamplight, my neck and breasts became as I remembered them at nineteen. He was so sweet—and so urgent, in the way that only a twenty-one-year-old boy can be. And I was the same, in the way that only a forty-year-old women imagining herself nineteen again can be. It was quite wonderful. And brief. I suppose I knew *something* might happen, so I made certain to have sex with my husband once or twice during those couple of months. Then—what was the war after World War II? Not that Korean one. Vietnam. Right. Trevor went to Vietnam a year later. That's where he died.

I went to the funeral with little Max in my arms, and Ruth and my husband by my side. Delores told me that Max was beautiful. "Must be from your side of the family," she'd said to me, very kindly. "He reminds me of Trevor when he was a baby." Then she wept so hard that her husband had to lead her away with both his arms wrapped around her body.

Certainly, if Max were still alive I would tell him all this—I would tell him that he got his red hair from Trevor. But he isn't. And Ruth, my Ruthie, has enough of her own puzzle to piece together. I just don't believe in all that "honesty is the best policy" nonsense. Sometimes it isn't—not with the people you love, anyway. When you come right down to it, the person you end up being in life is the one that the people you love *need* you to be. And that's enough.

I smell chamomile and lavender brewing. It must be the tea. Lavender is Winnie's favorite. See? In the short time I've been here, I already know that about her, which is more important than knowing whether or not she trained elephants or built skyscrapers when she was young. Winnie likes lavender tea.

"I didn't come here to do this," Eric says. "Nothing happened the way I thought it would."

"That's the way it is, sweetheart," Winnie says. "You plan a trip, thinking you know the reason for it, but until you reach the place you end up at, you never actually know why you went."

Smart lady. You listen up, Eric.

twenty-four

RUTH

Saturday afternoon. Two months to the day since we last "spoke." Hello. I'd be lying if I said that I haven't missed you all. I'd also be lying if I said that I have.

First: You already know this. Esther Andrea Sternberg died in her sleep. She was eighty-five. She wanted to go on one last trip, so we took a detour en route to my house and went to the desert to

Recent Posts:

- In Lieu Of

- Forgiving but Not Forgetting

- File Under: Failure to Launch

- The Upworthy Overdose

- If You're "Sober," What Am I?

visit Abbie, my daughter, Esther's granddaughter. She's so grown up now that you'd hardly recognize her. Esther wanted to be with Abbie in the desert. She also wanted to die there, which was, despite all my intuition and understanding, news to me. At the end, it was peaceful.

It was *nothing* like I expected it would be, even though it was like all the experiences I'd read about a hundred times over. She seemed to be in a deep sleep—in her body one moment, then not. First there, then gone. She certainly did not "rage against the dying of the light." That never was her style.

My telling of the last three months will be [relatively] short and sweet, like my mother would have wanted, because she never believed in giving out too much information, and I apparently gave out too much. In our search for the truth, in our attempts to nail down some sort of belief system, why does it always seem like we're compelled to one extreme or the other? *Absence makes the heart grow fonder. Out of sight, out of mind. No time like the present. Tomorrow is another day.* But I ask you, what's

- The Three Stooges Were Funny

About me:

I am your Humble Host and *First Mother of Blogging,* Ruth Sternberg, telling it like it is because that's all there is the adage for knowing the right amount of information? How much do you tell? What do you save? What do you erase?

We took a vacation together, Abbie and I, after the funeral. I promised Abbie that I'd keep the details private, as a personal memory between us, but I can give you a thumbnail sketch. We got on a plane carrying the lovely antique urn embossed with dolphins that we picked out for Esther's ashes. We *three* flew across the country to a body of water that shall remain nameless. Then we rented a car and drove back. At one point—and I think I'm allowed to say *this*—my daughter informed me that I seemed less angry than I'd ever been. At first that worried me, because I used to think that people who didn't regularly experience anger—those people who seem preternaturally inured to venting, who don't feel the need to scream at stupid drivers, listless salespeople, and careless children, who don't harbor resentment like it's gold bullion—were lacking in backbone, that they were emotionally repressed or just plain stupid. Now? Now I realize that they were simply smarter than me. It's not like those people don't know what anger is; they just know to filter that particular emotion from their hearts and minds, having concluded that anger is mostly a waste of time. Abbie is one of those people. Was she always smarter than me?

Oh, yeah, and a friend of Abbie's joined us on the last leg of our journey. But I'm not supposed to say anything more about *him*. Although I will tell you that I like him. He's cute, among other things. All right, I'm done with that. I promised.

Second: Thanks to the wonderful guest bloggers who filled in for me these last couple months. Go to their websites, sign up for their tweets, buy their books, fabulous women all. I know that Joy Bowden—author of the incredibly wise and funny *Put on a Happy F^#king Face: A Zen Guide to Finding Bliss (Without Botox) Over 40*—filled you in on my mother's passing, and, seriously, I read every one of your sympathy notes. More on that later. For now, a million, million thanks.

Third: And because nature abhors a vacuum, I lost Mom but found an old friend. Yeah, Missy, formerly known as "M," the "secret agent" of my blog (that's for you, Missy). She once was lost, and now is found—although, she actually found *me*. But I have to wonder: If that's the case, then maybe I was the one who was lost? Hmmm. I've discovered that she never meant to leave without saying goodbye, that she never wanted to disappear, that sometimes shit just happens that turns out to be greater than our resistance and longing and best-conceived plans. But I'll come back to this.

Fourth and last: On the drive back, right outside Oklahoma, we stumbled upon a yard sale. (Speaking of which, I'm abso-fucking-lutely excited to tell you that I'm a hundred pages into writing my first novel in twenty-five years, give or take. Real quick: It's a sci-fi thriller about the perfect mommy [Gwyneth, are you listening?] who meets an unexpected fate at an estate sale! I hope to be finished with the first draft by the end of the year. Shhhhh. But, yippee! Did I just say "yippee"? Okay, kill me.) The sale we hit was actually a *barn* sale, offering, unbelievably, several pairs of *authentic eighty-year-old Levis* that had been stuffed in the decrepit barn walls for insulation. I kid you not. I could've picked up the whole freakin' lot for a hundred bucks, because the owners obviously didn't know what they had. But I didn't do that. Instead, I told them that they could probably net at least ten grand for each pair. "Look it up on the internet—or have your grandkids look it up," I told them. Naturally enough, they were astounded. I have to say, though, I did pick up an authentic Tiffany lamp that was laying on a pile of hay, for like *a dime*. A saint I'm not.

twenty-five

ABBIE

To: FirstMother
Cc:
Subject: I'm here

Hi Mom,

I'm pretty much settled. That was sweet of
you to wanna surprise me with the matching
beanbag chairs, but they don't really fit in
my room, unless I throw out my bed. I'll
return them to Pottery Barn for some sheets
instead, if you don't mind. My roommate? She
seems nice, kind of punk with blue hair, but
she's from Venezuela and she's never heard
of you or me, so that's good. She loves '80s
music, so we've got that in common, although
she also likes Duran Duran. I guess I can

live with that.

I'm leaving for Miguel's funeral Friday night.
Eric's driving up on Thursday and we'll go
right after my orientation, so I'll see you
at Winnie's in the morning. I've got the
Sidney Sheldon piece picked out that I'm
going to read. I think you'll like it. I
just hope that I can get through it without
crying.

And, Mom, I really appreciate your asking my
permission to repeat the story I told you
about Claire and John McCain, but NO, you
can't repeat it, at least not until after
Claire dies, which could be a long long time.

I love you.

Alrighty then...

Ab

ACKNOWLEDGMENTS

You made it this far, dear reader. I thank you.

So very grateful to the friends who read this book in its earliest stages and gave much needed insight and encouragement: Marc and Susan Parent, Katya Shapostnik, Hope Perello, Margaret Hussey, Bernadette Sullivan, and Sascha Shutkind and her most eloquent teenage daughter, Sammy.

To Christine Moore, for asking me what I wanted.

To the art center SPACE, for allowing me to run with Personal Space, a reading series of local writers who never cease to inspire.

To Rick Szykowny, editor at *High Times*, whose editorial skills and expertise in things cannabis-related were invaluable in finishing this book.

To my whip-smart agent, Joy Tutela at the David Black Agency, for remaining enthusiastic about my writing for longer than most marriages last.

To Tracy Poust, chief commander of wit, empathy, and sanity, no matter the circumstances.

To my brother, Ken, and the women down through the Rizzos,

Sonkins, and Macdonalds, to whose strength and generosity I can only aspire to gain.

To Colleen Dunn Bates at Prospect Park Books, along with Patty O'Sullivan and Jennifer Bastien, for your seemingly tireless energy and imagination. You ladies are indie rock stars!

I'm beyond the beyond grateful to my children, Drake and August, who made me their mother. You are my joy.

To my husband, Jim Macdonald, as talented an actor and writer as he is the "camp counselor of fun," whose love and humor and kindness make everything sweeter. Love you madly.

BOOK CLUB TALKING POINTS

1. Our culture is full of parents who are certain that their kids should be famous. We see this in Ruth, who makes Abbie famous for merely existing. Why do parents do this? Is it all bad for the children or is there an upside?

2. Is internet or viral fame different than our traditional vision of what makes someone famous?

3. What is TMI? Are we all oversharing on the internet? Where do we draw the line?

4. Abbie and Ruth communicate via text and the internet, while Esther is not online and relies on conversation with her daughter and granddaughter for family news. In this digital world, should we encourage grandparents to plug in, or should we pull the plug more often and spend more time talking with our loved ones?

5. Abbie has a core circle of elderly friends, fascinating people who have lived full lives, had adventures, lost loved ones, and faced disease and other challenges. By assuming that our elders are Luddites, what kind of lessons are we missing?

6. It's easy to empathize with Abbie and Esther, but Ruth isn't a very sympathetic character. Which of her qualities are admirable? And did coming to understand Ruth's motivations make her more likable?

7. Would you want to be friends with Abbie, Ruth, or Esther? Why or why not? Do you find it hard to read about difficult protagonists in fiction?

8. Did any of your beliefs about mother-daughter relationships—or generation gaps—change after reading this novel? How so?

9. Ruth and Esther both harbor secrets—and guilt—that burdens their lives. Is lessening the burden of shame the upside of oversharing?

10. Abbie lies to her mother in order to achieve some personal freedom. Is it easier to lie in the digital age? And is it really a lie to create an internet persona like Ruth's? What separates truth from fiction?

11. What did you think about the major decisions that Abbie, Esther, and Ruth made about Esther's life? Was blogging about Esther's care selfish of Ruth? Was it wise for Abbie to "rescue" her? Were Esther's choices her own to make?

12. Is Ruth and Abbie's relationship changed for the better at the end of the novel?

ABOUT THE AUTHOR

Karen Rizzo is the author of *Things to Bring, S#!t to Do...and Other Inventories of Anxiety*, a memoir centered around her penchant for lists. Rizzo's stories and essays have appeared in the *Los Angeles Times*, *Salon*, *Fit Pregnancy*, and women's humor anthologies, and her plays have been staged at several theaters. *Famous Baby* is her first novel. She lives with her actor husband and their two children in Los Angeles.